COPYRIGHT

D1331703

THE YOUNG HEART

HELENA HALME

ONE

Helsinki, Autumn 1974

Kaisa was the new girl in town. Again. But she was well versed in entering a classroom where she knew nobody. At fourteen she had already changed schools no fewer than four times. During the past three years she'd spent exactly a year in each school. Still, there were a few butterflies in her tummy when she scanned the room full of new lanky students on the second floor of the redbrick building. It was late August and all the new faces, some looking up at Kaisa, had a healthy glow from the long summer, which was now nearly over.

Vappu Noren was the first girl Kaisa spoke to; she'd sat down at the desk next to her at the back of the classroom. Vappu was skinny, with an angular face framed by long, thin blond hair and a friendly smile. They exchanged a few words about how unfair it was to be back at school on what seemed like the hottest day of the summer.

Vappu said she, too, lived on Lauttasaari Island, where Kaisa had moved with her mother and sister Sirkka only a few weeks before. In fact, Vappu and Kaisa discovered they weren't too far from each other. On that first day, after they'd had lunch together, sitting on the grassy bank at the front of the school building, Vappu invited Kaisa back to her house.

Kaisa had no idea that Vappu's place was one of the large houses at the tip of the island, overlooking the sea. She'd walked along the shore with her mother after arriving in their new home, admiring the grand places, wondering what kind of people lived there. When she saw the Norens' house for the first time, she'd regretted her earlier, carefree, mention of the small flat she lived in with her sister and mother. The modern detached house had a vast wooden balcony at the front with a wide driveway below, leading to a garage on one side and a front garden with paving stones up to the door on the other. Kaisa's new home in Lauttasaari would have fitted into the Norens' large, open-plan living room. There were five bedrooms, a sauna, and a swimming pool next to a basement TV room. The lounge had floor-to-ceiling windows over-looking the sea. Kaisa tried to remind herself that, after the divorce, her mother had done well to get a rental on a two-bedroom flat in such a good area as Lauttasaari. The flat even had a partial view of the sea, if you craned your neck and looked to the right-hand side on the small balcony. It wasn't quite the same as the full vista of the Gulf of Finland, which the Norens enjoyed when they looked out of their living room windows, but still.

When she was ten, Kaisa's family had moved to Sweden from a small town in Tampere. It was 1970, and she and Sirkka were put into a large new school in a northern suburb of Stockholm. After her parents separated, she and her sister had moved with their mother to another part of the city, and her mother had found Kaisa a more centrally located school. Johanneskolan had been her favourite school, and just thinking about her lovely kind, teacher, Stefan Sorenson, made her want to weep, even though it was now over two years since she'd left. When her parents had decided to have another go at their marriage, the two girls and their mother had recrossed the Baltic to rejoin their father in Finland. To please them, Kaisa's father had rented a swish duplex apartment in Turku, with a sauna, two wide balconies overlooking the central cathedral and the rooftops of the old city. But after only a year, her father had been relocated again, this time to Espoo, near Helsinki, where both girls went to a local school.

Of course, the marriage didn't last. Both Sirkka and Kaisa could have told their parents this well before they reluctantly left their beloved Stockholm. The bitter fights restarted almost as soon as they moved back to Finland to 'become a family again', as her father put it.

Kaisa's parents finally divorced the summer after her fourteenth birthday. Kaisa and her sister then moved with their mother into the small flat in Lauttasaari and were sent to the local secondary school. Their mother insisted the school, in a modern low-slung redbrick building in one of the more affluent parts of Helsinki, would be far better for the girls than the one in Espoo.

'Lauttasaari is a nice area,' Kaisa's mother reminded her daughters when they grumbled about the lack of space in their new two-bedroom flat. She said the island suburb was where the well-heeled lived to be close to nature while also enjoying easy access to Helsinki city centre. In the small flat, both girls had their own bedrooms, but the lounge was divided into two, with an alcove for their mother's bed at one end and an old brown sofa at the other. This restricted the TV viewing in the evenings, because Pirjo decreed that the girls had to leave the room when it was time for her to go to bed.

'I need my beauty sleep,' she said. Their mother wasn't one for staying up late. She worked at Neste Oil, in a new high-rise office in Espoo. She had to take two buses to get to work, but said the money was good, and she needed every penny to bring up her two daughters.

'Since your father has decided to wash his hands of you two,' Pirjo said, and sighed.

'I don't want his money,' Sirkka replied. 'We're better off without the bastard.'

Vappu's parents had split up just like Kaisa's, but instead of having just the one sister, Vappu was the third child in a gang of four blond-haired siblings. Vappu was fourteen, just like Kaisa; her boyish, lanky, sports-crazy sister, Saija, was thirteen, her brother Erik seventeen, and the oldest, Petteri, had already turned twenty-two.

Petteri was serving his conscription in the Finnish army, so was rarely in the two-storey house that the Norens called home.

Visiting Vappu was a bit like going to a house party; there were always other young people there – Vappu's sister and brother Erik, and their friends. They'd all cram onto the large corner sofa in the basement TV room, or have sauna and pool parties, with illicit beer and *Lonkero*, the Finnish bitter lemon-and-gin drink that the girls liked. Sometimes even a bottle of *Koskenkorva* vodka would be passed around if Mrs Noren was working late, or out with her own friends. They'd grill sausages in the log-burner, which stood in the middle of the oblong basement room, and joke and flirt with each other. Kaisa liked Vappu's younger brother, Erik. He had pale blue eyes, straw-blond hair and a strong jaw. He'd just come back from a year as an exchange student in Minnesota in the States, and sometimes used American words, such as 'Yeah' and 'Alright', instead of Finnish.

During a particularly rowdy evening, when Mrs Noren was away on a weeklong conference, leaving Petteri in charge, a girl no one admitted to knowing threw up on the sauna floor. But the rowdy teenagers

took no notice of the quiet twenty-two-year-old
Petteri's attempts to restore order, so Matti, his best
and only friend, as far as Kaisa could tell, stepped in.
Matti, who stood out from the crowd of blond siblings
and their friends because of his dark hair and brown
eyes, took on the role of a grown-up. Acting like everyone's dad and speaking in a stern voice, Matti told the
guests to leave, and the Noren siblings to go to bed.
Kaisa stood there, staring at this adult amongst the
teenagers, a little drunk, not knowing what to do.
Vappu was very unsteady on her feet by then, and
walked slowly up the stairs, arm in arm with her
younger sister Saija, waving goodbye to no one in
particular like a queen on a balcony. She seemed to
have forgotten about Kaisa.

Matti bundled the unknown girl who'd been sick
into a taxi, and when he came back inside, Kaisa
noticed it was just the two of them standing in the
basement hall.

'I'll take you home,' Matti said in the same stern,
dad voice to Kaisa. He wasn't looking at her, and
Kaisa didn't want to cause any trouble, so she said she
could quite easily walk.

'It's past 2am, and I haven't had anything to drink,
you're safe with me,' Matti said with such confidence
and authority that Kaisa just nodded and followed
Matti out of the door.

On the way home in the car, Matti suddenly
turned towards Kaisa, and smiling said, 'You're a
good influence on Vappu, you know.'

'Thank you,' Kaisa said.

'She shouldn't drink alcohol, so it's good that you're no drinker either.'

Kaisa turned fully to see Matti's serious face, momentarily lit by the streetlights. They were about to turn onto the main road running through the western part of the island. Matti had stopped the car and was leaning forward, closer to the windscreen, to see if there was anyone coming from either direction. Kaisa thought about what he had said. Hadn't he noticed that Vappu was so drunk that she could hardly make it up the stairs to her bedroom? Or that Kaisa herself was quite the worse for wear?

'What do you mean?' she said, trying not to slur.

Matti turned to look at Kaisa. For the first time she noticed that his eyes were very dark and his lips very full. The street was absolutely empty, and the only sound came from the ticking of the indicator. The sky was black against the yellow glow of the streetlights. Matti's face was serious, but there was gentleness around his eyes when he replied, 'I shouldn't have said anything.'

Finally, Matti turned into the main road, and then onto the street where Kaisa lived. She had to direct him to the right turning, but apart from that they didn't speak for the rest of the short journey. When they reached her block, Kaisa got out of the car, and leaning in before closing the door behind her, thanked Matti for the lift.

'I'll wait to see that you get in safely,' he said smiling, and Kaisa nodded. There was absolutely no one about, so Matti's caution seemed unnecessary but strangely flattering. She waved to him from the door of her block of flats, and he waved back. She saw through the glass panel that he was sitting in his car watching her as she entered the lift. When she reached her bedroom and looked down at the dark road below, she half-expected to see Matti's car still parked below, but the street was empty.

In bed that night, Kaisa wondered how much Matti knew about Vappu's past. Her friend had confided in Kaisa that she'd fallen pregnant in the previous summer, and had been taken out of Helsinki to have an abortion in her mother's hometown, a small place near the Russian border.

'I got drunk one night and I don't even remember who it was,' Vappu told Kaisa.

Her friend had sworn Kaisa to secrecy, saying that only her mother and father knew about the abortion. Vappu said that even her sister and brothers thought she'd ended up in hospital because of suffering appendicitis while on holiday with her mother. In which case, who had told Matti about it?

TWO

One day after school, about two months after her parents' separation, Kaisa went to get her skates from the store at her old home in Espoo, where her father now lived alone. She'd been putting it off, but her class was due to go ice skating the next day and she knew no amount of excuses would get her off the hook with her new strict gym teacher. Besides, Kaisa didn't want to be the poor kid in class, who needed to borrow a pair of used, stinking skates at the ice rink. Kaisa liked skating and was quite good at it, so there was nothing for it; she would risk speaking to her father again. Luckily, she'd kept a key, and as she got off the bus and walked up the little hill to where the semi-detached, wood-panelled house stood, she saw the large windows were dark. Kaisa breathed a sigh of relief. She'd be able to slip inside, get the key to the store from the hook in the kitchen, walk to the end of the long garden, retrieve her skates and be on her way back to Lauttasaari in no time.

As she got closer to the house, Kaisa remembered the last time she'd seen her father. It had been early summer, the beginning of May. She'd just turned fourteen and her sister Sirkka was sixteen. Kaisa had been doing homework in her room when she heard her father calling their names. Their bedrooms stood side by side and opened off the oblong living room with its bright red carpet, which her father had promised to replace before they moved in but never had. When Kaisa opened her door, she was faced by Sirkka rolling her eyes at her. By then, Sirkka was living with her boyfriend in the centre of Helsinki most of the time, and was only at home by chance that evening.

'Sit down girls,' their father had said. He was sitting opposite the sofa, in one of the large comfy chairs, while their mother, her head bent down, was sitting in the other. A large man, with blue eyes and wispy light-brown hair, that evening their father's face was drawn and his eyes had huge dark shadows under them.

'Your mother has decided to leave me for the second time in our marriage,' he'd said, not looking at either his wife, or his daughters. 'And I suppose you two will choose to live with her again.' At that point her father had lifted his eyes at Kaisa, pleading with her. But Kaisa had moved her gaze away and glanced sideways at her sister, who shifted on the sofa and sighed. She knew Sirkka thought their mother 'had been crazy' to come back to Finland after she had left 'the bastard', as Sirkka often referred to her father. Sirkka hated their father, because he was always telling her what to do, or what he thought of her friends. They didn't agree on anything.

The first separation hadn't surprised Kaisa either. The fights and rows started in Stockholm shortly after the family moved there. When her father's two-year posting in the Swedish capital had come to an end, Pirjo and the girls had stayed in Stockholm while he went back to Finland alone. Both daughters had been glad to stay put. They'd learned to speak Swedish, and loved the city, with its bustling, international vibe. Pirjo rented a beautiful apartment near the Natural History Museum, with views over woodland, and only a bus ride away from Kaisa's new school and the lovely Mr Sorenson. Still, Kaisa was close to her father, and had missed him in Sweden, although she'd never told her mother or Sirkka this.

Coming back to Finland had been like taking a step back to a poorer, more inward-looking society. Neither Sirkka nor Kaisa had wanted to move to Turku, nor Helsinki a year later, let alone to the unfashionable suburb of Espoo, but they'd had no choice in the matter. Before the move, Sirkka had told her mother she was making a mistake, and back in Finland she'd barely spoken to her father, nor, towards the end, spent much time in the semi-detached house with the red carpet.

Now, as Kaisa slowed her pace, putting off going inside her old home, she shuddered remembering that awful day when her father had sat with his head bent, quiet for a long time. Kaisa had been afraid he would cry, but after the longest few minutes of her life, he'd given her a steady look, and said: 'OK, off you go with your mother. Good luck!' The last comment was delivered with a dry, sarcastic laugh. He'd then got up, put on his grey, padded coat and left the house.

When Kaisa opened the door to the house, a familiar, musty smell hit her. She'd forgotten that scent, which Sirkka claimed was mould. She said the three-bedroom, single-storey building was constantly damp and cold, because it had been built on a downward slope, with the red-carpeted lounge abutting the waterlogged garden. Their father had dismissed Sirkka's claims as 'pure nonsense', but now, faced with the familiar smell, Kaisa wondered if her sister had been right.

Kaisa closed the door behind her, and stepped inside the dark hall. The narrow, galley kitchen was right in front of her. She took a sharp intake of breath when she saw a large figure slumped at the table at the far end, in front of the window overlooking the garden. Her father turned towards Kaisa, and lifted his chin in a casual greeting, as if seeing her use her own key to come inside the house was an everyday occurrence.

When Kaisa got closer she saw her father had a glass and a half-empty bottle of *Koskenkorva* in front of him. He didn't seem too drunk yet, so Kaisa settled herself opposite him.

'I need to get something from the garden shed,' Kaisa said. Her voice was small, and she was struggling to find enough air to fill her lungs.

Her father lifted his eyes to Kaisa and said, 'Drink?'

'No, thank you.' Had her father forgotten she was only fourteen?

He looked down at his glass, lifted it to his lips and drained the contents in one go. He poured another glassful and said, 'No, I suppose your prissy mother has told you not to drink good old Finnish vodka?'

Kaisa's heart started to pound hard in her chest. She didn't dare reply.

'How is the fucking bitch?' Her father was now staring hard at Kaisa. His eyes were red-rimmed, and he had the dark shadows of a stubble on his chin.

'Look, I just want to get my skates, and ...'

'Yes, you want, all of you bloody women just want, want, want stuff all the time.'

Kaisa looked at her father, and suddenly, instead of fear, which his drunkenness usually provoked in her, she felt a surge of anger. It wasn't her fault that her parents weren't able to patch things up again in Finland.

'It's not my fault you are impossible to live with.'

She'd uttered the words before she fully realised they'd left her mouth. This was what her mother had said to her over and over during the long months they'd all lived together in Espoo. Kaisa could only agree; her father's domineering behaviour towards, not only their mother, but also Sirkka, and his constant drinking, weren't endearing him to anyone.

Kaisa's words had a terrible effect on her father.

'What did you say?' he boomed, getting up from his seat. His eyes were dark and his bulk towered above her. With horror, Kaisa saw him lift his hand as if to slap her, and thought that she should duck. But she couldn't move a muscle. His hand stopped a few millimetres from her face. For what seemed like an eternity, they stayed that way, her father with his hand close to her face, and Kaisa staring at him. She felt the tears running down her face before she realised she was crying, and angrily wiped them away with the back of her hand. Her gesture seemed to wake her father from the trance, and he slumped heavily onto the chair. Kaisa stood up, ran out of the house, and down the hill towards the bus stop.

THREE

The long-suffering Mrs Noren, whom Kaisa had been allowed to call Hilda, her first name, after she'd been friends with Vappu for a whole school term, worked full-time as a home economist at a nearby college, and as a consequence the Norens' house was filled with the delicious smells of home-cooking. But Hilda often complained about lack of money. To Kaisa, this seemed strange when she lived in a huge house with vast leather sofas, long glass-topped tables, and a basement full of expensive sports equipment of various kinds, from skis and skates to a large faded surfboard propped against the shower room wall next to the sauna. After the disastrous visit to see her father, Kaisa had borrowed a pair of skates lying unused in the cellar, and now she felt guilty about that. When Vappu had told her she could take them, Kaisa was sure her friend hadn't asked anyone's permission. Kaisa also worried about staying for supper so often, considering how Mrs Noren moaned about the cost of food. But Vappu, crossing her long legs just said, 'Don't mind Mum, she's just angry with Dad.'

The elusive Mr Noren owned a printing press in the eastern part of Helsinki, which Vappu and Kaisa sometimes visited after school. Just before Christmas, during the holidays, they worked for Mr Noren, stuffing envelopes with advertising leaflets. They earned a few marks for their efforts, and after a week's work, as a thank you, they were taken out to a nearby cafe for a cheap meal of breaded veal cutlet and chips.

Vappu's father seemed to lead a carefree, breezy existence, something Kaisa thought must upset Hilda, burdened as she was with looking after the four almost grown-up children, as well as her full-time job.

'He pays the school fees and the mortgage, and for food,' Vappu told Kaisa over the pile of advertising leaflets. Kaisa soon realised Vappu was her father's favourite, and having witnessed a few bitter arguments between daughter and mother at close hand, she also saw that this favouritism didn't go down well with Hilda.

When Petteri was on leave from the army, he spent most of the time in his room with his friend Matti, only emerging for meals and an occasional evening in the basement TV room. Vappu said her brother was the hermit of the family. He had large pale blue eyes and short, slightly darker blond hair. He preferred to sit in his room, reading, or cleaning his army boots and sorting out his uniform. One evening in the kitchen, while Hilda was cooking, Kaisa overheard Matti talk to her about Petteri's promotion to officer training, something which Mrs Noren seemed very proud of.

Matti often sat in the upstairs lounge quietly talking with Hilda alone rather than spending time with the younger children. Matti stood out from the crowd, not only because of his dark hair and brown eyes, but also because he seemed older and more experienced than any of them. For some strange reason, he seemed even older than Mrs Noren. He was already twenty-two, and seemed to know a lot more about life.

Once, towards the end of the school year, when Vappu sent Kaisa upstairs to the kitchen to fetch some lemonade, she saw a strip of light coming from Hilda's bedroom door, which was slightly ajar. She heard voices and realised one of them belonged to Matti. It was a few months after Matti had driven Kaisa home, and since then she'd noticed his eyes on her when they were watching television or sitting down to a meal. Still, he never really spoke to Kaisa, so she couldn't make out what he wanted from her. She thought perhaps Matti was worried about Vappu, or that Mrs Noren had asked him to keep an eye on Kaisa to see if she really was a good influence on her daughter. It all seemed very odd; surely it wasn't Matti's job to look after the Noren children? He was one of their friends after all.

So when she heard the voices, Kaisa's curiosity got

the better of her, and she moved a little closer to the door to listen to what was being said.

'She seems a good girl,' Mrs Noren said.

There was a brief silence, and Kaisa moved her foot so that she could change her weight quickly and make it look as though she was on her way to the kitchen if necessary, rather than listening in on a private conversation.

'So you wouldn't mind if I ...' Matti said.

'No, not at all,' Hilda replied quickly.

Kaisa strained to hear what Matti said next, but all she could make out was, 'That'll mean I won't ... anymore.'

She didn't hear Mrs Noren's reply, but Matti's voice was clear when he said, 'Well, goodnight, then.'

Kaisa could hear movement, and someone getting up, so she walked quickly away and was at the kitchen door by the time she heard the door to Hilda's bedroom closing.

'Hello!'

A moment later, Matti stood at the door to the kitchen. He smiled at Kaisa and came to stand very close to her. His dark eyes looked deeply into Kaisa's and she could feel her cheeks redden. Did he realise she'd been listening in on his conversation with Mrs Noren?

He was wearing a red-and-white checked shirt tucked smartly into a pair of brown trousers with firm creases at the front. Kaisa wondered why he never wore jeans, and realised the checked cotton shirt was the most informal, or fashionable, piece of clothing she'd seen him in.

'Hi,' she said and began opening and shutting cupboard doors, looking for the lemonade.

'Is this what you're after?' Matti said and brought out a full bottle from the large, two-door American-style fridge, which Kaisa thought epitomised the luxury in the Norens' house.

'Thank you,' she said and took the bottle from Matti's outreached hand. Their fingers touched. For a moment, rather than letting go of the bottle, Matti held onto it, while looking into Kaisa's eyes, 'Can I get anything else for you?'

Kaisa lowered her eyes and shook her head. She walked out of the kitchen. She could feel Matti behind her, and her mind was spinning. Was Matti flirting with her? His behaviour had changed after he'd driven her home that crazy night of the nauseous girl, but he was so much older than her; surely there were girls he liked closer to his own age? Kaisa had overheard Petteri tease Matti and say something about Matti fancying someone. She'd assumed he meant Vappu, and had thought it funny; Vappu had told Kaisa many a time that she thought Matti was 'a boring old man'.

Then there was the conversation Kaisa had just overheard. Had Matti been talking about her to Mrs Noren?

But why?

FOUR

Helsinki, Midsummer 1975

Matti knew it was a gamble to stay behind in Helsinki for Midsummer, and when he told his mother she was most put out. Luckily, he was rescued by Aunt Bea, her mother's younger sister, who had offered to take mother to the summer cottage in the Turku archipelago in Matti's place.

'A young man needs to be with people of his own age,' she'd said, giving Matti a certain look of understanding. Of course, his mother hadn't taken it at all well, but eventually his aunt whispered something in his mother's ear and, giving Matti a startled look, his mother had said, 'Ah, I see.' Her dark brown eyes had looked sad, but she had nodded and let the matter drop.

His mother was still not happy about leaving her

son alone in Helsinki for a whole weekend, and spent the days before Midsummer sniping and giving instructions to Matti on how to look after the house. Matti was on leave from his army conscription, and a nagging mother was the last thing he needed.

'When you are here on your own, you must remember to lock the doors properly,' she said, talking to Matti as if he was planning an orgy in her immaculate house while she was away. When she told Matti to remember to wash the sheets of his bed 'afterwards', Matti nearly lost his temper. Instead, he said calmly, 'Mother, please don't; you've gone too far.'

That had made her stop, but she still had a hurt look on her face when Aunt Bea came to fetch her on the day before Midsummer's Eve.

Of course, Matti fully understood the real reason why his mother was upset. Ever since the death of his father when Matti was fifteen, they had spent Midsummer at his aunt's place in the archipelago rather than in their own summer cottage by the lake in Haapamäki, just North of Helsinki. It had become a tradition, which kept his mother's thoughts away from that awful Midsummer's Eve when his father had collapsed and died at the cottage. Aunt Bea had lost her husband in a car accident a year earlier, so the two sisters were able to comfort each other.

When Matti bundled his mother into the front seat of his aunt's car, his ten-year-old twin cousins excitedly waving at him from the back, he had felt sorry for her and a little embarrassed. He stood at the door, making sure his back was straight, waving to his blond-haired cousins, ignoring the thought that his mother knew – not exactly what he was planning – but at least the nature of his scheme.

It was funny really, because his mother hadn't stopped talking about him not having 'a special female friend'. To protect his mother, and any future wife, he'd not wanted to bring a girlfriend home. He needed to be absolutely sure first. There had been one possible candidate – Sanna, a brunette he'd dated for a whole year at school. She would have been perfect daughter-in-law material with her Swedish-speaking background. Her father was a company director and her mother stayed at home to look after two children who no longer needed looking after. Matti wondered if he would have married Sanna if she hadn't left him on the day of their Baccalaureate graduation. That was five years ago now, and since then there had been no serious relationships. The women who wanted to do it with him were often older than him. He knew he acted more mature than his years, but that was something he felt proud of. He'd had to become the man of the house at fifteen, quite suddenly, and his mother had begun to rely upon him the way she'd relied upon his poor father.

He thought about the island in Turku archipelago now as he drove through the empty streets of Helsinki towards the old Lauttasaari bridge. The weather was perfect for Midsummer. The thermometer fixed to the outside of the living room window had shown 20 degrees when Matti checked the windows before leaving home, as per his mother's strict instructions.

The sun was high up in the sky, and his aunt's island would be bathed in sunshine. The sea, though cold so early in the summer, would be perfect after a hot sauna.

Matti's aunt was an excellent cook, and he was sure the food and the schnapps served in the evening would be delicious . With the help of the twins, Aunt Bea would now be building the stack of twigs and wood for the Midsummer pyre, ready for when the sun got closer to the horizon. There'd be other fires visible from the opposite shores. His aunt's cottage at dusk was one of the most beautiful – and romantic – places to be on Midsummer's Eve, the darkened sea stretching out to the shores of other islands dotted with fires as far as you could see, and the sky above a pale grey, never growing fully dark. They said Midsummer was a magical time in Finland and now, making his way past the industrial edge of Helsinki mainland, from where the Lauttasaari bridge jutted out towards the leafy island suburb, Matti was counting on that being true. He'd decided that he wouldn't take Kaisa to his mother's house in Munkkiniemi, but would try to get an invitation to her flat instead. He had packed a small overnight bag – just in case – with spare shirt, a set of underwear and a toothbrush.

The first time Matti had set eyes on Kaisa was on a cold September day nearly a year before. He'd been with Petteri in his room, listening to the new Deep Purple LP his friend had bought. Knowing Matti only listened to old Finnish 1950s music, tangos and slow waltzes, Petteri had tried to convince him that heavy rock was something he'd like. Petteri was on weekend leave from the army, and while Matti wasn't at all interested in the new LP he did want to know how his friend's first few weeks of conscription had gone. Petteri, characteristically, just said, 'It's OK.'

Matti had deferred his service because he was studying for the entrance exams of a forestry course at Helsinki University. It was famously oversubscribed; in a country covered in forests, everyone wanted to study how to look after them. Matti had already applied and been rejected twice, so this was his last chance. He spent ten hours a day in the University library in the centre of town, poring over the books set for the exam, as well as working on various mock exam questions he'd managed to obtain through a friend of his aunt. But unlike most young Finnish men, he was also looking forward to doing his military service, and intended to go into the army straight after the exam in May. He hoped, like Petteri, he'd be good enough to make it as far as officer training – which was why he needed to find out as much as possible about the army from his friend. But instead of talking about his experiences, Petteri had got up, carefully taken the LP off the turntable, put it back in its colourful sleeve and said, 'You staying for dinner?'

Matti nodded, and together they made their way across the landing to the kitchen.

The Norens' house, unlike Matti's own home, was always full of people. Friends of the Noren children seemed to have an open invitation to come and spend the evening, or stay overnight, at any time. Mrs Noren would just sigh when told so-and-so was staying for dinner. She would lay another place on the kitchen table and add more potatoes to the pan to feed the growing army of teenagers.

That evening, with the harsh sounds of Deep Purple still burning his ears, Matti had seen the new girl sitting at the end of the table, timidly looking at Mrs Noren, who was talking in a loud voice about how tired she was and how much all this food she was serving was costing. No one, apart from the new girl, had been listening to her rant.

'Hello Hilda,' Matti had said, partly to stop the nagging, and partly to attract the attention of the girl. When she lifted her head Matti had felt winded by the blue eyes that gazed straight at him. She had blond wavy hair, which came down to her shoulders, and there wasn't a trace of make-up on her face. She wore a tight stripy jumper, revealing small, pert breasts. 'She's the one, she's the one, she's the one!' The words had rung in his ears, thumping to the beat of his heart. Looking around, he'd wondered if anyone had noticed. The buzzing in his ears had been so strong, surely the others must have heard? But everyone, apart from the girl, still staring at him, had been talking at once. Vappu, whose friend Matti assumed the girl must be, because Hilda's middle daughter was sitting next to the beautiful creature, was arguing with her younger brother, Erik, who was holding onto something high up above his head, preventing his sister from getting at it. Fed up with fighting a losing battle,

Vappu turned to her friend and the girl's gaze moved away from Matti. He was surprised to find that no one else had noticed the current running through him. Even Petteri, standing behind him had been oblivious, and impatiently nudged Matti's back and pushed him into the kitchen proper. Matti had taken a seat at the bench, opposite Petteri's younger brother Erik, the lanky seventeen-year-old, whom Matti presumed girls found attractive. He had pale blue eyes and a mop of thick blond hair, which he had a habit of touching and running his long fingers through. Matti supposed he'd learned that move from his time in America. He'd acquired a whole new set of gestures, most of them attempts to convey a more confident boy, during his exchange year in Minnesota. Erik had also become taller than Petteri, and Matti, and cocky with it. Petteri was stronger though, so he could still put Erik into a headlock and bring him in line, but in front of girls the boy showed off. The crowd around the table had been unusually small that night – apart from the new girl and Matti there were none of the usual waifs and strays.

'Hello, I haven't seen you here before,' Matti said, directing his words towards the girl. He'd made his voice steady, ignoring his heart rate, which was still racing.

Vappu lifted her head, and before the new girl could speak, said, 'Kaisa, Matti, Matti Kaisa.'

Vappu giggled, and the new girl, Kaisa, joined in, sending Matti a cursory glance to acknowledge the mock-formal introduction.

After the meal – savoury mince with boiled potatoes and Hilda's excellent home-made pickled cucum-
bers – Matti sat on Petteri's bed and ran through one
of his textbooks for the university exam. Then Petteri
said, 'She's good-looking, isn't she?'

'Who?' Matti felt a dread in his guts, but kept his
eyes on the economics of good forestry maintenance.

'The new girl, Kaisa.'

Matti was quiet for a moment, collecting himself.
When calm enough, he said, trying to sound noncha-
lant, 'Oh, I didn't notice.'

Petteri and Matti's eyes met for a moment, and
then they both looked away. Petteri leafed through a
music magazine, with his back to Matti. After another
quiet moment, he said, 'You won't mind if I have a
go, then?'

'Of course not,' Matti said, quickly. Too quickly.

As Matti drove along the empty streets of Lauttasaari,
his thoughts turned once again to the Norens. The last
time he'd been to see his best friend Petteri, he had
missed supper because they'd spent longer at the
shooting practise than planned. When he dropped
Petteri home, he'd accepted his friend's invitation to
come and have a bite to eat upstairs in the Norens'
kitchen. But when he'd got to the top of the stairs in
the modern, two-storey house he'd been intercepted
by Petteri's mother. She'd been standing by her
bedroom door at the far end of the large lounge,
wearing her pink velveteen dressing gown.

'Matti, can I have a word,' she'd said.

Petteri had shrugged his shoulders, saying nothing. His friend's reaction wasn't unusual, and was one of the reasons Petteri and Matti had become such good friends at school. They both believed that if you had nothing important to say, there was no need to speak.

Matti saw he couldn't ignore Mrs Noren, even though he was hungry, so he nodded to Petteri and walked across the parquet floor of the darkened living room and stepped inside Mrs Noren's small bedroom. Hilda, as Matti had called her for years now, slept in a small room at the far end of the house, separated from the hustle and bustle of the teenagers that filled the villa. As always when they talked in low voices, Matti sat next to her on the bed, the only light coming from a small lamp. A window facing the sea filled one whole wall, and Matti saw that the wind had got up and formed white-edged waves on the surface of the water. Turning away from the window, he looked at Hilda's face. Matti was by now used to being the broad shoulders on which older ladies cried. There was his mother, of course, but before that his aunt had often called at his house when his parents were out, in need of comfort.

Not that Hilda was that old; she was only in her mid-forties, but life hadn't treated her well. As Matti listened to her account of Mr Noren's latest indiscretion, he thought how with a little effort Hilda could look quite attractive. She was a good fifteen years younger than his own mother, and was sporty and slim, so the only thing holding her back was her obsession with her ex-husband. Mr and Mrs Noren had divorced three years previously, after he had an affair with his secretary. He was now living with the twenty-five-year-old and their young son.

'He is so insensitive and unthinking. He knows full well I couldn't buy Vappu brand-new sunglasses, these fashionable Ray-Bans that she's been nagging me for. He took her shopping at Stockmann's.' Hilda lifted her pale grey eyes at Matti. He could see she'd been crying; her make-up had left smudges on top of the puffy skin under her eyes. Matti put his arm around Hilda, and squeezed gently. She blew her nose on a lacy handkerchief she had in her hand, and continued. 'I mean, he has to understand that now the others will want new sunglasses too, and I can't afford three new pairs of Ray-Bans. Have you seen how much they cost?'

'I'm sure Petteri won't want a pair, and I doubt Erik …' Matti said soothingly.

Hilda put her head on Matti's shoulder and sighed. 'Yes, I know that, but the principle of it. He can't just go and buy an expensive thing like that for one of his children and ignore …'

'Shh,' Matti said and lifted Hilda's chin up. He looked into Hilda's sad eyes. He knew how to comfort Hilda, and knew that was why she'd called him into her room. They had agreed to end it weeks ago, but Matti knew Hilda needed him. He'd stop as soon as Kaisa agreed to go out with him. He planted a gentle kiss on Hilda's lips, which felt cold and thin, and warmed them with his own mouth. Her body relaxed, and she moved her hand onto his crotch. Matti peeled the thick dressing gown off Hilda's shoulders, revealing a thin see-through nightie. He pulled his own jumper and shirt off quickly, and pressed his chest against Hilda's full breasts. Her body was warm and soft. Hilda placed her hands on Matti's cheeks and, pulling him down to her bed, whispered, 'You're a lovely young man, do you know that?'

During the Midsummer weekend in June, Kaisa was alone in the flat in Lauttasaari. The Norens had gone to their summer cottage by a lake in Eastern Finland, and Kaisa's mother was visiting a friend somewhere in Northern Finland. Sirkka was away with her latest boyfriend. Kaisa had been invited to go with Vappu to their cottage, but she had chosen to stay and work in the R-Kiosk in the small shopping centre on the island, a job she'd found after the school term finished at the end of May. She couldn't take time off, not when she was supposed to be the holiday cover for the other staff; besides, she needed the money. She'd be working on her own through the holiday weekend, something she was very pleased about. Her manager, an old woman who wore lipstick far too bright for her narrow, tight mouth, had told Kaisa that she was the best summer worker she'd had in the kiosk, and trusted her to look after the shop for the three days. The hours were shorter because of the holiday, and Kaisa didn't have to open up until 12 o'clock on Midsummer's Day, so at least she could have a lie-in on Saturday. The whole kiosk, including the back room and toilet, wasn't bigger than her bedroom. It sold mainly newspapers and sweets, but they also carried a small stock of toiletries and household goods such as washing-up liquid and tampons.

The most fascinating items for Kaisa were the many men's magazines, which she had to sort out with all the other printed material, packaging up old issues in the small back room and replacing them with new magazines when they arrived. While she did this, when the shop was quiet, she sneaked a look inside. The pictures of naked women, mostly lying on their backs, their pert breasts topped with pink nipples, and their legs spreadeagled to show the dark-haired nether regions made Kaisa tingle. She wondered if being aroused by pictures of naked women meant something was wrong with her, but then when, on occasion, the pictures showed a man entering the woman, with his hand on her breasts, or between her legs, Kaisa could feel herself wanting to be that woman. So far she'd only had fumbled encounters with boys. She'd once been fully naked with a boy when quite drunk, but nothing had happened, and afterwards she felt ashamed that she had gone so far with a stranger. It had happened before she'd come to Lauttasaari, at a house party with some of Sirkka's friends from the Espoo school. Kaisa hadn't even told Sirkka about what she'd done with the boy, and wanted to forget all about it afterwards.

When she looked at the pictures, Kaisa's thoughts turned to Erik, Vappu's younger brother. A few weeks before, when at last he'd noticed her, he'd asked her to come to his bedroom during one of the party nights at the Norens' house. But instead of trying to kiss Kaisa, he'd told her about a girl he'd left behind in America. He showed Kaisa a picture of Kimberly, which he kept on his bedside table. She had perfectly blow-dried brown curls falling onto her shoulders, a wide smile revealing an even row of white teeth, and sparkly eyes that looked straight at you. She was in a typical American pose, her body half-turned towards the camera, revealing a slim, erect figure with two perfectly formed breasts under her school jumper. Kaisa knew she had no chance competing with the American beauty, and was in equal measure puzzled and flattered by the occasional attention Erik continued to show her even after telling her about Kimberley. He'd still tease Kaisa about the way she ate a sausage, for instance, or tried to sneak a look into the sauna when it was Vappu's and Kaisa's turn to bathe.

SIX

A t last Matti was able to make his move on Kaisa. It had taken many long months. Out of courtesy to his friend, who seemed oblivious to his silent gesture, he'd held on and not approached her. But luckily he had patience. Only once during that time had he taken it upon himself to give Kaisa a lift home after a particularly messy party, but even then he'd not made a pass and instead waited to see if Kaisa liked his friend better. At last, in February, a full five months after they had set eyes on Kaisa, Petteri had told Matti that he'd driven Kaisa home on the back of his Honda motorcycle, trying to impress her, no doubt, with his new purchase. When they'd arrived outside her block of flats, he'd turned off his motorbike. 'Kaisa, you must have noticed I like you,' he said.

Kaisa hadn't replied, so Petteri continued, 'So I wondered if you'd like to be my girlfriend?'

Making sure there was no show of emotion in his voice, Matti asked, 'What did she say?'

Petteri didn't look at Matti, but at the floor. 'She said, "No".'

Matti hadn't wanted to grill his friend for more details of the incident. Besides, knowing Petteri, he wouldn't say anything anyway. Inside, Matti felt jubilation, and immediately started planning his own strategy. He'd first have to square it with Hilda, then slowly, almost imperceptibly, he'd start to woo Kaisa.

The opportunity, when Kaisa was alone in town at Midsummer, had come as a gift from God. By chance he'd heard Vappu and Kaisa talking about summer as they sat tanning themselves on the Norens' front lawn. Because Petteri was now working full-time at his father's printing press, and Matti had entered the army, Matti's visits to the Norens' house were rarer. He had taken to making all sorts of excuses to pop by when he was on weekend leave, to bring Hilda some women's magazines his mother had finished reading or some other small gift his mother thought Hilda might like. Although the two women had met only a handful of times, they liked each other and Matti's mother felt sorry for Hilda for 'having to bring up all those children on her own'. It was on one of these impromptu visits in June that Matti had overheard Vappu's disappointment on hearing that her friend would be working over the Midsummer holiday.

'And you'll be all alone in your flat!' Vappu had exclaimed.

Now, parking his car around the corner from the

kiosk, Matti allowed himself to daydream about a future with Kaisa. If his gamble worked out, he and Kaisa would never again miss seeing the nightless night on his aunt's island. He would teach Kaisa the ways of the world; he was more than seven years older and would look after her.

Walking up to the kiosk, Matti thought how blond Kaisa's hair looked. It was longer than he remembered. The light, curly strands, escaping from behind her ears, where she'd tugged them out of the way, framed her face and made her pale blue eyes, now gazing up at him, seem even bigger.

Matti's mouth had become dry, and he had to swallow to make any sound at all. 'I thought you'd like some company for Midsummer?'

Kaisa was a little surprised, too taken aback, he guessed, to say anything. Instead she smiled sweetly and looked down at her hands.

'What time are you free?' Matti asked and moved closer to the window where Kaisa stood, on the other side of the counter, slightly above him. She was wearing a short-sleeved frilly blouse, with little holes in the fabric. Matti could see the taut bronzed skin underneath.

'Four o'clock,' she said quietly, and this time her smile was directed straight at Matti.

He glanced at his watch. He had overheard Kaisa tell Vappu that she could close the kiosk early on Midsummer's Eve.

'That's good,' he said, and when she still didn't speak, added, 'I thought we could go to Seurasaari

Island. They have dancing there and light the Midsummer pyre out at sea later. It will look spectacular.' Matti knew that Kaisa had only moved to Helsinki the autumn before, whereas he was a *barefoot Hesalainen*, born and raised in the city. He would show Kaisa the town, although he preferred the countryside; built up areas depressed him if he spent too much time in them. He loved hunting in the woods, but he would tell Kaisa about that later. Tonight was all about Midsummer in the city.

SEVEN

The island of Lauttasaari was deserted on the morning of 25th June, Midsummer's Eve, when Kaisa stepped out of her block of flats and stood by the pavement to wait for the number 21 bus. There were no cars about at all, and when the bus turned up it was empty, and remained so all the way to the small shopping centre in Lauttasaari. It was a warm morning, with the sun already high up in the sky, concealed by a thin layer of clouds. Kaisa felt sad and lonely; she should be out of town, enjoying herself by a lake somewhere, instead of working in the boring R-Kiosk, which she knew would have only a handful of customers that day, most of whom would be either too old or too poor to leave town. There would be the odd drunk asking if they sold low-alcohol beer (which they didn't), or some party-goers buying mixers to have with their vodka.

As it turned out, Kaisa had counted just two

customers by lunchtime. She sat down on a seat in the back room, from where she could keep one eye on the counter. She decided to read a women's weekly that had come in the day before, and eat the rye and cheese sandwiches she'd prepared at home. She was too depressed about her own sad loneliness to even look at the sex magazines. Midsummer was supposed to be the time when young women like her fell in love – not sitting at the back of a kiosk ogling dirty pictures of naked men and women.

Kaisa jumped when a familiar voice said, 'I thought I'd find you here.' She'd been engrossed in an article about decorating a table for Midsummer, with her head bent. She lifted her eyes up to Matti, who was leaning over the counter. He had a wide smile on his face.

'What are you doing here?' Kaisa stood up and went over to the counter. She was so surprised to see his face, she could feel an involuntary furrow of her brow.

'Aren't you pleased to see me?' Matti said, his smile fading.

'Yes, but is something wrong?' Kaisa was thinking of her friend, Vappu. She had been unusually quiet as Kaisa sat in her room watching her pack a holdall for the holiday. 'I hate that place,' she'd said, but their conversation had been interrupted by Mrs Noren ordering Vappu into the car. The two friends had hugged and Kaisa had promised to write. Vappu was going to be away most of the summer, while Kaisa stayed in town and worked in the stupid kiosk. But why would Matti know anything about her friend? He was supposed to be away in the army.

Matti regarded Kaisa for a moment, then smiled again. 'No, nothing. I was in the neighbourhood, and thought I'd pop in to see if you were working today.'

Kaisa wracked her brain. How did Matti, the sensible friend of Vappu's oddball brother know she was working in the R-Kiosk?

'Oh,' she said.

They were both quiet for a moment. Matti was still gazing at Kaisa. Next his eyes fixed on the shelf behind her. As if remembering something, he said, 'Can I have a packet of Café Crèmes, please?'

Kaisa suppressed a smile as she turned around to pick up the old-fashioned small cigars Matti smoked. Vappu made fun of Matti with his cigars. She rolled her own smokes, and was forever running out of cigarette paper and picking pieces of tobacco from her lips. Kaisa didn't really smoke, but had the odd cigarette if she was offered one. Smoking was a good way to hide your nerves in company; it gave your hands something to do. She wondered if she should buy a small pack of Marlboro herself. She could smoke them on the balcony, while she drank the two bottles of *Lonkero* she had saved for herself. What a way to spend the nightless night, she thought.

When she was counting the money at three-thirty, the intake from only five customers, including Matti at lunchtime, Kaisa wondered if she was doing the right thing; she'd never thought of Matti in that way before. She'd been so surprised by his invitation to spend Midsummer Eve with him that she'd agreed without thinking too much about it. To go and see the pyre at Seurasaari, and do a bit of old-fashioned dancing, with an old friend (or friend of a friend's brother!), was preferable to sitting and drinking a *Lonkero* alone on the balcony.

Matti stood waiting in the warm, bright sunshine when Kaisa stepped out of the kiosk and closed the heavy back door behind her. She gazed at the boy, or man, in front of her. He was wearing green trousers and a flower-patterned shirt through which Kaisa could see his taut upper body. He stood very straight, like a soldier. He was just about the same height as Kaisa. His dark hair was short like that of the boys you saw skulking around in their Finnish army uniforms in the city, or at the central train station, kissing their girlfriends goodbye on the platform before boarding the train. The haircut made Matti look even older than he was. Of course, he had a full seven years on Kaisa's fifteen, but that didn't worry her. She'd always considered herself more mature than her age; she'd spent so much time with her older sister and her friends that she felt her true age was more like seven-teen, or even eighteen.

Matti took hold of Kaisa's hand and smiling said, 'You ready?'

'Yes, but can we go via my place? I need to get changed.' She was wearing a pair of jeans and a white top, but having spent all day in the stuffy kiosk, she felt grubby and needed a shower.

Matti grinned, and Kaisa wondered if he thought that was an invitation.

'Of course,' he said, his eyes fixed on Kaisa.

'You can wait in the car,' she said and removed her hand from his.

During the drive through the empty Lauttasaari streets to her flat, when neither of them spoke, Kaisa began to realise that this was a date. A proper, grown-up date. When she thought about it, she hadn't seen Matti with a girl, nor had she heard that he'd ever had a girlfriend. He probably didn't ask girls out very often. It occurred to her that she might be the reason he was in town: to be with her. At first the thought flattered Kaisa, and even raised a small smile to her lips, but now she felt a terrible sense of responsibility; what if the date didn't go well? She hadn't thought of Matti in a romantic way over the year she'd known him; on the other hand, there was something fascinating and dangerous about him. He seemed so much more grown-up than Vappu's eldest brother, and his friendship with Mrs Noren made him seem apart from the rest of the gang in that chaotic house. Kaisa remembered how safe she'd felt with him that time he'd taken her home in his car. She knew he was dependable.

When they got to Kaisa's block of flats, she opened the door and said, 'I won't be long.'

Matti looked at her and nodded. His face was serious, and Kaisa wondered, as she darted up to the door and into the lift, if he was annoyed with her.

When she emerged, having changed into a floaty cotton dress with matching espadrilles, both of which she'd dyed pale lilac in the bath, Matti was standing by the car, leaning on the bonnet and smoking one of his little cigars. He gave Kaisa an appreciative glance, which made her blush. The canvas shoes had a small wedge heel, and were tied at the ankle, which made Kaisa's legs look even longer than they were. When she'd given herself a final glance in the hall mirror, she'd been pleased with the way she looked. Her blond hair reached her shoulders, and the sunny weather over the past month had bleached it into a straw-blond that suited her. She walked slowly up to the car, conscious of Matti's eyes on her, but unable to meet his gaze.

He threw his cigar on the pavement, crushing the stub with his shoe, and opened the car door for her.

'You look nice,' he said, as he sat down at the wheel.

Kaisa returned his smile, but said nothing.

'Seurasaari, here we come!' Matti said and Kaisa laughed. There was also something comical, yet endearing about Matti. He obviously wanted to impress her with his cigar smoking and his flower-pattered shirt.

Matti had brought the smell of the cigar into the car, making Kaisa think of her father, and Christmas, which was the only time he smoked cigars. While Matti drove, images of the happy holidays of her childhood flooded her mind. She hadn't seen her father since the incident at the old house, and the memory of his face, and his hand so close to slapping her face, made her shiver. Her thoughts were interrupted when Matti turned the radio on and slipped in a cassette. An old-fashioned tango, called 'A Tale of Brown Eyes', began playing.

'I like Finnish dance music,' Matti said.

Kaisa glanced at his profile and wondered what kind of time warp she'd fallen into. This was music even her mother thought passé; something her grandmother listened to. But the melancholic singing seemed to suit the occasion, and Kaisa's mood, and she found herself swaying to the music as they passed over the old Lauttasaari bridge, turned into Mechelininkatu, and then into a smaller road flanked by large villas on one side and the sea on the other.

'You can't quite see it, but over there is President Kekkonen's residence,' Matti said when they were crossing the footbridge to the Seurasaari island after parking the car. He pointed right towards thick woodland, where the red roof tiles and the yellow top floor of a large villa were just visible. Kaisa had never been to this part of Helsinki, and when Matti realised this, he took her hand and led her towards a path. He told her all about the island of Seurasaari. They investigated the insides of small moss-covered cottages, where, he said, their ancestors had lived. 'Seurasaari is an outdoor museum,' he said proudly, as if he'd come up with the idea himself. But he was born and bred in Helsinki, Kaisa thought, so she guessed he had the right to be proud of his own city.

He was still holding her hand when they got to a

freshly mowed meadow. In the middle stood a band-
stand, and a few people were scattered around, mainly
couples sitting on blankets and drinking beer or something stronger straight from the bottle. The field led
down to the water, where Kaisa could see the unlit
Midsummer pyre jutting out from the end of a long,
ancient, wooden jetty. Kaisa had noticed Matti take a
bag from the boot of the car, and he now took a
blanket out of the bag and spread it on the grass, in an
empty space next to a large birch tree. He pulled out
two bottles, one of *Lonkero*, which he opened and
handed to Kaisa with the words, 'You like this, don't
you?', and one of Sprite, which he clinked against
Kaisa's *Lonkero*. 'Happy Midsummer!'

Kaisa drank the bitter lemon gin drink. Even
though it felt strange to be drinking alcohol while
Matti was having a soft drink, she was glad Matti had
thought about the drive home. He was so responsible,
and mature, she thought.

When the band started playing, Matti took Kaisa's
hand and led her to the old wooden dance floor. The
sun had moved down towards the horizon, but even at
six o'clock it was still full daylight. Long branches of
young birch trees had been fixed to poles around the
stage, making the small clearing in the middle of the
wooded island seem magical.

Several other couples had already started dancing,
and were moving around the stage with expert steps.
Kaisa wasn't very good at a tango, or a waltz, but

when the simpler, faster dance, the Finnish *humppa*, came on she managed a little better. Kaisa felt she was a real grown-up woman, and looking around at the other couples, she noticed she was the youngest there. But no one needed to know that she was only fifteen. Matti was a confident partner, and once Kaisa had relaxed a little, she found their bodies fitted well together. One of Matti's strong arms held Kaisa's waist, making sure she moved in the right direction. When the band began playing another tango, Matti pulled Kaisa closer. She felt the increased heat of his hand through the thin fabric of her cotton dress and the pressure of his muscular thigh push between her legs. During the dance, when he suddenly changed direction, Matti turned his face towards her, his brown eyes burning into hers. Kaisa melted into them and felt giddy with the smell of his aftershave mixed with something musky. She lowered her eyes and saw the dark stubble on his chin. When her cheek accidentally touched his, the sharpness of the bristles burned her skin.

She found that her shoes weren't the best kind for the dance-floor – the wedge heels were too stiff – so after a few numbers she asked Matti if they could stop for a while.

'Of course,' Matti said, letting go of her and bending the upper half of his body in an old-fashioned bow. Kaisa lowered her eyes. He made her think of Russian plays she'd seen with her mother, or the TV adaptation of *War and Peace* that her mother had loved so much. Taking her hand again, Matti led her to their blanket by the birch tree. She was aware of the tautness of his body and the fullness of his lips, as he lay opposite her on the blanket.

'I'm sorry, I don't really know how to dance,' Kaisa said and turned her head towards Matti. She was sitting cross-legged, with her skirt tucked underneath her legs to preserve her modesty.

'You dance beautifully.' Matti's voice was hoarse. He was lying on his side, looking up at Kaisa, supporting his head with his hand. One of her knees touched his taut tummy, and when Kaisa shifted her body to remove it Matti placed his hand on her thigh to keep her in place. His touch sent a violent shiver down her spine. His slender fingers were close to the secret place between her legs. Their eyes met and Kaisa wondered what his full lips would taste and feel like. His eyes were pools of brown liquid, and she felt herself sinking into them. Then she suddenly remembered Matti was Petteri Noren's friend. His best friend. Petteri, whom she had snubbed when he'd asked her to be his girlfriend. It had been the strangest thing; a few months previously, Petteri had given her a lift home on the back of his new motorbike. When they'd arrived outside her block of flats, Kaisa had been handing him the spare helmet that he kept in the small container at the back when he blurted out, 'Kaisa would you like to go out with me, and be my girlfriend?'

She'd been so surprised that she'd laughed; but seeing the expression on his face change, and his mouth tighten into a straight line, she'd quickly said,

'No, sorry.' Like a coward, she'd fled towards the door to the flats and not even waited for the lift in case he could see her through the large window in the entrance. She'd run up the stairs and only felt safe when she was inside the flat. She'd felt embarrassed about her reaction. She'd behaved like a little girl, not thinking how he must have felt. She should have explained that she'd never thought of him in that way, and that as Vappu's older brother he felt like family to her, though she did have to admit that she'd rarely spoken directly to Petteri during all the months she'd spent in the Norens' house. He was either away in the army, or sitting in his bedroom with Matti, listening to noisy hard rock records.

'Why don't you lie down next to me, Kaisa,' Matti said, his eyes boring into her.

Kaisa said nothing, but stretched her legs out and laid slowly down, pulling her skirt so that it covered her bottom. Matti lifted his hand while she arranged herself on her back. He moved closer to her and placed his hand gently on her waist. She couldn't take her eyes off Matti's face, and when he gently moved his lips closer to hers she closed her eyes and let him kiss her.

Nothing could have prepared Kaisa for how she felt when he held her in his embrace and kissed her, pushing his tongue inside her mouth, possessing her. Neither of the two boys who had put their lips onto hers, while clumsily fumbling with her bra, had made her feel like this. They'd been rough, sometimes missing her mouth altogether, more concerned with trying to get their hands underneath her clothes. But now she wanted to abandon herself to this boy – or man. She wanted to press her body harder against Matti, but he stopped and breathlessly said, 'Shall we go somewhere more comfortable?'

EIGHT

Matti took Kaisa to his house, which was only a few minutes' drive away, even though he'd previously decided against doing this. She was so lovely and the way her body quivered underneath him when he kissed her on the blanket in Seurasaari made him impatient. In the car, he told Kaisa his mother was away, and that they could have the whole house to themselves.

'Oh,' she replied, now quiet beside him on the passenger seat, where his mother usually sat talking incessantly about the other cars and the appearance of people walking along the pavement.

Minutes later he parked the car, carefully placing it in its usual spot, dead centre in the drive, so that there was enough room for both driver and passenger to alight onto the paving slabs (his mother complained if she had to step onto the grass with her good shoes). He had a great urge to pick Kaisa up and carry her inside, but she remained seated, even when he stopped the engine and said, 'Here we are!'

She smiled at him briefly, then looked at the hands on her lap. It occurred to him that this might be her first time. He needed to get her inside quickly.

'Come, I'll show you my room.' He was now standing outside the car, carrying the basket containing the blanket and the drinks he'd taken with him in one hand and holding the passenger door open with the other. He gazed down at her, noticing her slender neck, how strands of blond hair curled behind her earlobe. He wanted to bend down and touch those hairs and kiss her neck, but Kaisa wasn't moving. Instead, she still had her head bent, looking away from him.

Matti placed the basket on the paving slabs, touched Kaisa's chin, making her turn towards him.

'What's the matter?'

'Can you take me home, please?'

Matti stared at Kaisa, but she said nothing more. He glanced briefly at his watch and saw it was only half past seven. It was still light, the sun was just above the roof of the house. There was plenty of time, he told himself. He saw he'd been too keen, trying to get to her too fast.

'Of course – I'll just drop this off inside. You could come in to have a quick look at the house. That wouldn't hurt, would it?'

Kaisa gazed at him as if to assess his honesty. Her big blue eyes were so lovely, and her lips, slightly apart, so inviting, that Matti had to fight another urge to kiss her. He smiled, and said, 'But if you'd rather wait in the car, that's no problem. I just need to nip in quickly, and then I'll take you home.'

She seemed to consider his words.

'OK,' she said and got out of the car.

NINE

Matti parked his car outside her block of flats, turned off the engine and shifted on his seat to face Kaisa. 'Here we are.' His eyes were dark, and a smile was hovering around his full lips.

Kaisa was feeling very guilty. She'd had a nice time with Matti in Seurasaari, and she knew he'd taken great care to make sure she would enjoy herself. It seemed he'd planned the whole day just to show her Midsummer Eve in the city, but they hadn't even seen the fire being lit out on the water. And when they left early, she knew what he'd wanted to do with her, and she had wanted it too. But when they'd got to his large house in Munkkiniemi, it had begun to feel weird being there with him. Suddenly she just wanted to go home. Matti had said his mother was away on some island of his aunt's, far in the Turku archipelago, and had persuaded her to come inside to wait for him while he dropped off the picnic things. Still, she couldn't relax in his house. He'd been very under-standing when she'd asked to be driven home, and had let her wait in the large living room with its shiny parquet floor, old-fashioned furniture and huge chan-delier hanging from the high ceiling. He'd shown her where his room was, but she'd just looked in from the doorway. All she could see were posters of guns on the walls, a large desk with thick books on it by the window, and a single bed, neatly made up, along the wall. The room had a scent of something strong and very male, and it had made Kaisa feel odd; a mixture of being scared and excited.

'You sure you wouldn't rather sit here and talk for a bit,' Matti had said, standing behind her. Matti had placed his hand on her waist, where it burned through the thin fabric and caressed her bare skin underneath. She'd turned around and suddenly they'd been in an embrace. Matti bent down and kissed her. His lips had tasted of toothpaste and Kaisa realised he'd been to the bathroom and brushed his teeth.

'That's so considerate,' she'd thought briefly, and then Matti had pushed his tongue inside her mouth, pressing his body hard against her. Kaisa had felt his erection against her thigh, and had felt a desire to just abandon herself, just let go, and let Matti do whatever he pleased with her. But something had stopped her. Whether it was the large empty house, so alien to her with its antique furniture and polished floors, or Matti, being so old and experienced, she didn't know, but she'd pushed him away, saying, 'Sorry.'

'You drive a man crazy,' Matti had said and let out a long breath.

Kaisa had asked him to take her home, and he'd picked up his car keys from the hall table next to a pink telephone, and they'd got back into the car again.

Now sitting in the car, side by side, outside Kaisa's block of flats in Lauttasaari, Matti said, 'I like you very much, Kaisa.' He lifted her chin with his hand.

Kaisa looked into his eyes, which were kind, but still dark and full of desire.

'And I'm serious about you.'

Kaisa felt herself falling into those eyes. He bent down and kissed her again, more gently this time. His mouth tasted less of toothpaste, and his lips were softer. After what seemed like an age, Matti pulled away, and still holding Kaisa's chin, said, 'I've fancied you ever since I first saw you.'

'Really?' Kaisa managed to say, even though she was still breathless, still in a dream-like state after that kiss.

'And I'm going to marry you, Kaisa Niemi,' Matti said and smiled.

TEN

Helsinki, Summer 1980

Matti's room in the house in Munkkiniemi was full of guns, and posters about guns. When they had first started going out, he'd tried to show Kaisa how to load a pistol, but she was too scared even to hold it in her hand for more than two seconds. She now shivered when she looked at the technical chart on how to assemble a hunting rifle, which Matti had pinned to the wall above his bed. She knew Matti took gun safety very seriously, and all his licences were in order. She knew the rifles he owned were all stored in his wardrobe, and his three handguns, one of which was a Russian antique, were tucked away inside their cases in the top drawers of his desk. But still.

Over the five years they'd been together, Matti had

often tried to explain his fascination with firearms to Kaisa, but when she still couldn't understand he would just squeeze her tightly and say, 'My little bird, you're too delicate and sweet for the way of the world.'

She was now sitting alone on his bed, on top of the green crocheted bedspread, waiting for him. He said he needed to talk to his mother before she went to bed. It was only just past six o'clock, and Kaisa had arrived straight from the KOP bank, where she'd started working as a summer intern at the end of May. She had just finished her first year at Hanken School of Economics. Matti's mother had been watching TV in her room when she arrived. Nowadays Mrs Rinne spent most afternoons in bed because her rheumatism had become much worse in the past six months. Matti was very worried about her, Kaisa knew, which made what she had to ask him much more difficult. Kaisa sighed. Why had she promised her mother and sister that she'd go on holiday with them before she'd asked Matti? The truth she knew was that Sirkka had backed her into a corner during their telephone conversation the previous evening. Her mother and Sirkka had already booked a villa in the Åland Islands. 'It's equal distance between us, a perfect place for us to meet!' Sirkka had said when she'd come to the phone. It was true, as Sirkka had pointed out, that they hadn't spent any proper time together for ages, not since she had moved back to Stockholm with their mother in October. The Christmas they all spent in Stockholm in her mother's small flat seemed a long time ago. It was now mid-July, and Kaisa couldn't think of anything nicer than to spend a week with them in a cottage by the sea. She straightened her back when she heard footsteps outside the door.

Matti came to sit next to Kaisa and started kissing her.

'Mother is nearly asleep, but we have to be quiet,' he whispered in her ear.

Kaisa let Matti take her top off, and fondle her breasts. She sighed with pleasure and decided to ask Matti about the holiday later.

'Why Åland?' Matti said afterwards.

They were lying in Matti's single bed. Kaisa was resting her head on Matti's bare chest.

'The islands are between Finland and Sweden, I suppose, but I don't really know.'

'I can't take any time off work now, not when I've just started,' Matti murmured, adding, 'so I'm sorry, I don't think we can go.'

Kaisa was quiet for a while. Now was the moment.

'I was thinking of going on my own.'

Kaisa could feel his chest muscles tense underneath her cheek. Matti got up abruptly and quickly put his pants back on. He stood still for a moment, in front of his wardrobe with his back to her. His head was bent.

'I haven't seen either my mum or Sirkka for a long time.' Kaisa said.

Matti didn't reply. He continued to stand there, with his bare back to Kaisa. He opened the wardrobe where the rifles were just visible, in a straight row behind his clothes, which hung in an orderly fashion, trousers at one end and jackets and shirts at the other. Matti grabbed a shirt with a swift action, sending the empty hanger rocking back and forth.

'I see,' he said, turning around to face Kaisa. His eyes were dark and he had his hands on his hips. His back was so straight it looked as if he'd arched it. His upper body was still bare, and he was holding the green-checked shirt in his hand. The hem and cuffs were trailing on the floor. Kaisa thought how well she knew each contour of his body. How many times she'd touched that sleek, wide, hairless chest; how often she'd unbuttoned those trousers and taken hold of him, giving him pleasure. But now, with him standing there, right after they'd done what they'd done on his bed, trying to be quiet through it all, avoiding the squeaks they knew the bed could produce if too much weight was placed in the centre, she felt tired. She realised what he wanted was to own her. To control her life. Kaisa thought of all the guns he owned. What he was doing now was holding a gun to her head, demanding she stay in Helsinki with him, telling her that if she didn't ...

'It's not as if I'm going somewhere like Tenerife with my girlfriends,' Kaisa said, keeping her voice level, trying not to show the anger that she was beginning to feel. What girlfriends?, she thought, and let out an involuntary snort. She never saw any of her friends anymore. Between studying at Hanken, and now working at the bank, and being with Matti, there was no time to see anyone else. The number of times she'd cancelled a date with Vappu, she didn't care to remember. Now Vappu had all but given up on her, hardly phoning her anymore. Kaisa looked down at her hands and took a deep breath. She didn't want to have an argument; she was tired of arguing, although she kept thinking how unfair Matti was being. Just because he couldn't take a holiday, she wasn't allowed to have one either. Not even one with her mother and sister!

'You think this is funny, do you?' Matti said. He was now fully dressed and had gone over to sit at his desk by the window. The light outside had faded a little, and as he flicked his desk lamp on, it lit Matti's face from the side. Kaisa saw the twisted contours around his eyes and mouth. Seeing him in pain like that made Kaisa's heart soften. It wasn't easy for him, she knew. Between looking after his mother, his new job in the customs office at Helsinki harbour, and his disappointment at failing to get into university to study his beloved forestry management (he'd taken the entrance exams three times), Matti was under pressure. His mood wasn't helped by the fact that after finally being accepted into a business college, his last back-up plan, Kaisa had got into the prestigious Hanken at her first attempt. After four years she would have a degree in economics, while Matti would only have a certificate in business studies. Kaisa had heard her fellow students at Hanken call the place where Matti studied in the evenings 'a secretarial college'.

Kaisa got up, pulled her T-shirt over her head and put her knickers back on. She went over to Matti and took his head into her hands. 'It's my mother and sister, and it will only be a week – seven days, that's all.' Kaisa tried to kiss Matti, but he turned his head away.

ELEVEN

Matti insisted on driving Kaisa to Helsinki airport, even though he had to swap his shift at the Customs House. Kaisa tried to be less annoyed with him; she knew he was only looking after her. As she sat in the front seat of his old green Opel Kadett, his mother's car, she felt guilty for looking forward to a whole week without him. She'd been surprised that, in the end, Matti had agreed to this holiday with her mother and sister in the Åland Islands. He'd asked her several times how much it cost, even though her money had nothing to do with him. If one of the women in the bank hadn't tipped her off about the student discounts the airline gave she would not have been able to afford to fly. Instead, she would have had to take the train to Turku, and catch one of the Swedish ferries to the Åland Islands. It would have meant a journey lasting the best part of a day, whereas on the mid-morning flight she'd arrive in Mariehamn, the capital of the islands, just before 11am. Kaisa leant back in the car and closed her eyes. In a few minutes' time she'd be at the airport, on her own, free with her own thoughts.

'How can your mother afford to rent a big holiday cottage in Åland?' Matti's voice startled Kaisa. She'd dozed off, and was half-asleep, dreaming of the holiday. She'd been sitting on a sandy beach, with the sun shining from a bright blue sky and water lapping at her feet.

Kaisa turned to her fiancé. 'She has a good job in Stockholm.'

'Hmm,' Matti said, his voice full of scepticism.

Matti, and his well-bred, wealthy mother, had been suspicious of her divorced mother from the beginning. Kaisa remembered the awkward questions the first time her mother and Sirkka had met Mrs Rinne.

Matti and Kaisa had been engaged to be married for almost two years before she'd invited Kaisa's mother and Sirkka for coffee at the house in Munkkiniemi, the diplomatic quarter of Helsinki, close to where President Kekkonen had a summer residence. Kaisa hadn't minded that her two worlds had been kept apart; Matti's life at home seemed to belong to the 1950s, with its Finnish dance music, crystal chandeliers and French rococo-style furniture. The thought of Matti's mother visiting the small flat in Lauttasaari with its tiny rooms, or seeing the kitchen, with its old table that her mother had painted black to go with the pattern of the curtains, which had large red, yellow and purple flowers on a charcoal background, filled Kaisa with dread. She could hardly imagine what Mrs Rinne would have made of the fish netting, complete with starfish and coloured polystyrene floats hanging off the ceiling in the living room. One of Sirkka's boyfriends had found the netting and given it to them. Where it came from, Kaisa had no idea. On a rainy Sunday afternoon, Sirkka, Kaisa and their mother had decided to nail it onto the ceiling for fun, just to see if it would brighten up the otherwise dull-looking room with its brown sofa and white walls. Looking at the unusual decoration after they'd finished, Kaisa'a mother said, 'At least it's not conventional. If it starts to smell, we'll take it down,' she added, and the netting stayed. On days when Kaisa was on her own in the flat, lying on the sofa, looking up at the starfish, she wondered if a fisherman was missing his net.

The designated day of the meeting between the two families was a sunny Saturday in early June. Matti had offered to collect the three women from their flat in Lauttasaari.

'Lauttasaari is as good an area as Munkkiniemi,' Kaisa's mother had said as they waited for Matti's car to turn into the road. Kaisa didn't comment; they all knew this was blatantly not true. Sirkka let out a snort and turned her pretty blond head towards Kaisa. Their mother, who looked even younger than she usually did, in her knitted close-fitting dress, which came just above her knees, revealing her shapely legs, continued to gaze out of the kitchen window, ignoring her daughters.

As they'd sipped the hot black liquid from Matti's mother's delicate bone china cups, sitting on the pink chintz sofa (Matti's mother's favourite colour was pink), Kaisa felt the tension in the room.

'It's very kind of you to invite us to your beautiful home, Mrs Rinne,' Kaisa's mother said.

Kaisa looked at her mother. She seemed completely at ease with the bone china cups, the chintz and the chandelier casting an odd sparkle over the room on such a bright summer's day. Why were the lights on in here, Kaisa wondered, but lowered her eyes towards Matti's mother, who, looking at Kaisa, but speaking to her mother, said, 'Please call me Aila.' Without smiling, she'd added, 'We're going to be family soon, after all Pirjo!'

Sirkka glanced sideways at Kaisa and they both suppressed a smile. Matti's mother had swiftly assumed a socially superior position, and had called Kaisa's mother by her first name without asking, while giving permission to be addressed by her first name. It was true that Mrs Rinne was much older than Sirkka and Kaisa's mother, and looking at Pirjo in her slightly too short knitted dress, you could have easily mistaken her for the bride-to-be. At 39, she looked more like a woman in her early thirties, and was often mistaken for an older sister.

It was also true that Mrs Rinne was titled, a descendent of a Russian aristocratic family, who had changed their name after the revolution to avoid being recognised by the Bolsheviks and sent back to Russia. Matti said she talked too much about the old days, and the houses in 'Mother Russia', and the position her family had once held there. 'She's never set food on Russian soil,' he said on the rare occasions he criticised his mother in front of Kaisa.

Matti's mother, incapacitated by her rheumatism, had a large frame, but delicate features, in spite of the puffiness Kaisa guessed her illness, or medication, caused. She had thin, grey-blond hair, carefully coiffured, and wore a pale pink cardigan over a wool skirt and silky blouse. Mrs Rinne always wore fine jewellery; today, around her wrinkled neck she had a string of real pearls that matched a pair of small drop earrings.

Kaisa knew her mother and Sirkka had made an effort for this first meeting with her soon-to-be mother-in-law. Sirkka, for once, wore a sensible skirt and blouse, while her mother had opted for the lilac knitted dress. It suited her well, bringing out her feminine figure, but Kaisa's pride over how good her mother looked was mixed with fear that Mrs Rinne would find her all together too young and attractive for a mother of her prospective daughter-in-law.

When they'd arrived, Matti's mother had ushered them all into the lounge, where a girl, her weekly help, had served coffee with three kinds of biscuits and a three-tiered cake, which Kaisa knew Matti had collected from one of the expensive bakeries in town that morning.

When the girl came in and served the cake, Matti's mother asked, 'And what does Kaisa's father do?'

Aila delivered the question unsmiling, with minimum movement of her lips, which puckered as she waited for a reply.

Surprised at the sudden mention of her ex-husband, Kaisa's mother looked up from her plate, and a little flustered answered, 'Oh, he's an engineer.'

Mrs Rinne nodded her approval, and Kaisa breathed a sigh of relief. At least something in her family came up to scratch.

'But you are divorced, am I right in thinking that?'

Kaisa's mother put down her plate and, looking squarely at Mrs Rinne, or Aila, said simply, 'Yes.'

'You must be proud of your daughter, however,' Mrs Rinne continued and smiled at Kaisa.

Kaisa's mother turned her face towards her youngest daughter and said, 'Very.'

Kaisa had just found out that she'd been admitted to the Swedish-language School of Economics at Hanken, and she guessed this was the real reason why Mrs Rinne wanted to meet Kaisa's mother and sister. The common joke was that Hanken was the place where all the rich Swedish-speaking boys and girls went to learn how to run the country.

As Kaisa sipped coffee in the airport café overlooking the runway, waiting for her fight to Mariehamn to be called, she thought how well it suited Mrs Rinne that her future daughter-in-law would be a Hanken graduate; that way she could pretend to her friends that Kaisa was really from a good Swedish-speaking family, instead of the daughter of a common garden Finnish divorcee. Kaisa shook her head; she was being mean. Matti's mother was overpowering, her beliefs were old-fashioned, but she wished nothing but well for Kaisa and Matti. Kaisa didn't understand why she'd been feeling so resentful of Matti and his mother lately. She was grateful for being able to rent a flat at a very favourable rate from Matti's aunt; it helped her a lot while she was studying and had only her loan, a small allowance from her father and income from her part-time work to draw on. Did her resentment have anything to do with the approaches of a certain wealthy Swedish-speaking boy at Hanken, she wondered?

TWELVE

The Åland Islands, Summer 1980

K aisa had never been to the Åland Islands
although she had passed them many times
while travelling on the ferry from Finland
to Sweden. When Sirkka had phoned Kaisa and
suggested it would be the perfect place for them all to
have a holiday, Kaisa had been excited. Although the
islands were much closer to Stockholm than they were
to Helsinki, they belonged to Finland. The population,
however, was fiercely independent and firmly Swedish-
speaking. That was no problem to Kaisa; she'd learned
Swedish while at school in Stockholm, and now she
attended a Swedish-speaking university. Both her
mother and Sirkka were fluent in Swedish too. They
had moved back to Stockholm the previous autumn,
leaving Kaisa to her studies at Hanken.

'You have Matti, after all,' her mother had said.

While flying low over the Finnish archipelago, Kaisa admired the beauty of this, her native land. As the Finnair plane began to make its decent, the islands came into sharper focus. The sun glimmered on the clear blue surface of the sea, and she could see densely wooded islands scattered with red, wooden buildings and straw-coloured fields. Here and there, Kaisa spotted rows of hay bales, or a herd of cows grazing. Everywhere the landscape was broken up by water, with wooden jetties protruding from small inlets.

Kaisa's mother and Sirkka were waving at her in the low airport building. They looked tanned and relaxed. Sirkka's mother had booked a cottage for two weeks and they'd already spent five days on the islands. The hugs seemed to go on forever, but eventually, grabbing her bag, Sirkka said, 'So you escaped, Little Sister!'

'It wasn't like that,' Kaisa said, grinning.

'C'mon girls, we need to catch this bus!' Their mother pointed towards a blue and white coach, which had its engine running. The three women sprinted towards the vehicle, where a grumpy-looking driver sold them tickets and pulled out into the road before they'd all sat down. They giggled like schoolgirls as they struggled, nearly losing their balance, to find seats. The other people in the bus smiled at them; it was tourist time, the end of July, and Kaisa felt happy and free. She looked at her mum and Sirkka in the seat in front of her, both in their summer dresses, their heads bent towards each other, studying the timetable for the next bus to the cottage from Mariehamn, the main town. Their already fair hair was bleached by the sun and the sea.

'There's a few minutes' walk from the bus stop at the other end, but we can manage, can't we girls?' Kaisa's mum said and her daughters nodded.

'Unless we walk across the fields, but our mum is afraid of the cows, so we'd better not!'

Sirkka began a long story about their second day in the cottage, when they'd decided to take a short cut to buy provisions from a little shop by the side of the main road. They'd come across a small herd of cows. Their mother had started running, encouraging the younger cows to follow her. Letting out little screams of fright, she'd escaped across a broken fence, straight into the arms of the farmer, who happened to be the owner of the holiday cottage.

'They don't bite,' he'd said, and smiled.

'I was so embarrassed!' their mother now said. 'What must he think of me!'

Sirkka nudged her mother and said, 'Quite a lot, I should think.' She raised her eyebrows at Kaisa, which made her giggle again.

Though a little annoyed at being teased, Kaisa could see her mother was pleased; she shifted on her seat, pulling her shoulders back. 'Don't. Bo is just a very well brought up man.'

While she'd been running, one of her kitten-heeled shoes had got stuck in a cowpat. The farmer,

Bo Gustafsson, had calmly walked across and retrieved the shoe, shooing the eager cows away with his arm. He'd even cleaned it expertly with a piece of cloth from his pocket, and handed it back to Pirjo.

'Luckily, the shoe was only soiled at its heel, and mother was able to walk to the shop, although the stink was unmistakable,' Sirkka laughed. She turned her face towards Kaisa, 'But enough about our mother's love life, how is Matti? Still as jealous as ever?'

Kaisa didn't have time to answer. At that moment they arrived in the centre of Mariehamn, and people around them started to gather their things and leave the bus.

The wood-clad cottage, painted bright red, which Sirkka and Kaisa's mother were renting, looked like the ones she'd seen from the window of the plane and was just what Kaisa had hoped for. It was situated at the end of a winding lane, which ran past a larger, pale yellow two-storey house set on a small hill, which belonged to the farmer. A field of teal-coloured rye, gently bending in the breeze, formed a backdrop to the cottage, while the porch at the front overlooked the sea. A rickety looking jetty cut through the pale yellow reeds, which grew tall by the shore and then reduced to a few wispy stems sticking out of the surface of the sea. The path between some leafy trees and the water-side led to the sauna, Sirkka and her mother told her excitedly. Changing out of her sandals and into a pair of tennis shoes, Pirjo asked, 'Shall I go and put it on?'

'Yes!' both daughters said in unison, and Kaisa saw her mother disappear down the path.

The cottage had a large living room with a kitchen set into a corner and a wood-burning stove against one wall. There were two bedrooms; Kaisa was to share the larger of the two with Sirkka. The cottage wasn't at all overlooked; it stood just below a bank that led down to the sea, and Kaisa's thoughts turned to what she'd learned about the Ice Age at school; it was the reason this beautiful landscape existed, she thought. She took in a deep breath and relaxed.

'*Lonkero*?' Sirkka said, holding out the familiar blue-and-white labelled bottle. She was grinning widely. 'Just like old times?'

Kaisa took a swig of the drink, and returned her sister's smile. Drinking like this with her sister reminded her of the period after they'd moved back to Finland from Stockholm, when Kaisa and Sirkka had got into the habit of going out together at weekends. They hadn't had any friends in their new school in Turku to begin with, and their age difference of two and half years hadn't seemed a problem. Besides, during their parents' separation, the two girls had grown closer to each other. When they moved back to Finland they'd both been underage, but armed with fake IDs they had gone to clubs none of Kaisa's new classmates would have dared enter. But when her sister left school at eighteen, and Kaisa met Matti soon after, all that had stopped. Now, at the age of twenty Kaisa felt as if such irresponsible partying was far in her past. She was a grown-up woman. An adult engaged to be married.

'I've been dying for you to come over. It's no fun going out with your mother!' Sirkka grinned. 'And it's Saturday night.' Sirkka looked sideways at Kaisa. 'Shall we sample the delights of Mariehamn tonight?'

THIRTEEN

The cottage had no telephone, but Pirjo told Kaisa she could telephone Matti from the main house. When Kaisa made her way up past the rye field, she noticed how quiet it was. Bo Gustafsson was a little surprised to find Kaisa on his doorstep, but once she'd explained she wanted to make a quick phone call, he smiled and invited her in.

But Matti didn't seem at all glad to hear from Kaisa.

'Everything alright?' he said, his voice cold and strained.

Kaisa sighed. She didn't want to argue with him.

'I just thought you'd like to have this number in case you need to get in touch with me,' she said.

She very nearly hung up on him, when he didn't reply, but added instead, 'I can't talk for very long, I'm calling from the house of the farmer who owns the cottage.'

'OK, Matti said, and added, begrudgingly, 'have a lovely time.'

'See you next week, then,' Kaisa said. She put down the phone and stood still for a moment, thinking how tired she was. She'd not been able to sleep the night before for worrying about being late, that Matti would make up some excuse not to take her to the airport and she'd have to struggle on two buses.

'Everything as it should be?' Bo Gustafsson asked. Kaisa turned around and saw the farmer standing in the middle of the kitchen. His pale grey eyes were gazing at Kaisa from underneath a pair of bushy, light-coloured eyebrows. Kaisa smiled, and said there was no problem. She thanked him and tried to give him money for the phone call but Bo refused. Her mother was right, he was a very nice man, she thought, and walked slowly back to the red cottage.

After a long, hot sauna, and a swim in the sea, Kaisa could have just lazed in front of the fire with her mum, but Sirkka insisted on going out.

'You sure you don't want to come?' she asked her mother, who had settled on the sofa with her book.

'Quite sure! You two go and have fun.' Her mother smiled. She was wearing a summery dress, her blond hair still wrapped in a towel and her cheeks flushed from the sauna and the swim. She had a book on her lap. 'I'm going to have an early night.'

Sirkka had large pink rollers in her hair, and was waving a drier over them. 'We're going to miss that bus if we're not careful. I can't afford a taxi there and back!'

On the way into Mariehamn, Kaisa and Sirkka giggled like two teenagers. They'd had another couple of *Lonkeros* in the sauna, and Kaisa felt a bit tipsy.

'Let's go to Club Marina first of all, then to the Seglarklubben on the other side of the strip, where the Swedish boys usually go, and then the Arkipelag,' Sirkka said. She gave Kaisa a sly look, 'When did you last go out *without* Matti?'

Kaisa looked at her sister. She'd been unsettled by the phone call with Matti. Still, she didn't want to let Sirkka know there were any cracks in her relationship. 'Last week,' Kaisa lied.

'Oh yeah, to work you mean?'

'No, actually to the cinema with Vappu.' Again Kaisa lied. She'd planned to go, but then at the last minute Matti had changed his nightshift at the Customs House, and Kaisa had cancelled. Vappu hadn't been best pleased, but Kaisa couldn't do anything about that. She couldn't leave Matti on his own.

'That must have been hard to get past him!'

'Don't make fun of me,' Kaisa said.

'I'm not, not really.' Sirkka hugged her sister and for a moment the two sat silently as the bus pulled into the town.

It was barely past 9pm and Mariehamn was busy with revellers.

'It's like being abroad!' Kaisa said to Sirkka when they sat down with their drinks at an outside table in the Club Marina in the East Harbour. Helsinki had one outdoor place, the Happy Days café in the centre of town, but it was never as busy as this. This place overlooked jetties moored with beautiful sailing boats of various sizes. There were a few smaller motorboats too, as well as one large yacht. There was no wind, and the sun was setting over the harbour, reflecting the shapes of the masts onto the glass-like surface of the water. Kaisa was admiring the view, thinking how satisfying it would be to be a painter who could recreate the scene in front of her, when she heard voices.

Kaisa saw him before he saw her. He was almost a head taller than anyone else in the place, but she would have recognised him from his broad shoulders anywhere. Kaisa turned to her sister and was about to say something, when he caught her eye. He was smoking a cigarette at the bar, looking at her. There was a smile hovering over his lips, but Kaisa wasn't sure if it was meant for her. She kept her expression neutral, but her heart was beating fast underneath her blouse.

'Who's that?' Sirkka said, leaning over the table to Kaisa.

Kaisa shook her head, 'No one.' She didn't want to give Tom, 'the rich boy', the satisfaction of knowing that they were talking about him, although Kaisa wanted to tell Sirkka all about the guys who'd approached her and her new friend Tuuli during their first week at university.

The exchange between Sirkka and Kaisa was interrupted by two younger guys, wearing matching red polo shirts with yellow lettering, who stood by their table, blocking the view to the bar. They looked the sisters up and down and Kaisa lowered her eyes, trying to signal her unavailability to them. But they began talking to Sirkka. One had straw-blond hair and was slimly built, and the other was a little shorter with brown hair. They were asking − in Finnish − if they could share the table with them.

'Yes, of course,' Sirkka said, sending a sideways glance to Kaisa.

Judging by their accent the boys were from Helsinki. They carried a glass of beer each, and as they sat down, the blond one introduced himself. 'I'm Lasse, and this here is my mate, Jasku.'

Kaisa took the proffered hands and told them her name. She saw that the T-shirts bore a name of a sailing club in Helsinki. 'You sailed over?' she asked. She knew this was the most common way for wealthy Finns to come over to the islands. Although Åland was further away from Finland than Sweden, there was virtually no open sea between the islands and mainland, especially if you went up north via the coastal town of Turku.

'No, but we're crewing a mate's boat here,' Lasse, the blond one, said. He turned towards Sirkka and added, 'What about you, do you sail?'

'No,' said Sirkka, 'but we don't mind being passengers.'

It was past 1am by the time the sisters were in a taxi on their way back to the cottage. They'd met several men, but as Sirkka put it, either they were 'too young, or too full of themselves' to interest her. Kaisa, of course, wasn't looking for a boyfriend, so she just went along with what her sister wanted to do. The 'young sailing boys', as Sirkka dubbed them, from the Marina, had wanted Sirkka and Kaisa to go with them to Arkipelag, but Sirkka said they'd agreed to meet a friend in another place.

'That's OK, we'll come with you.' Lasse had said.

Sirkka had regarded him for a while, and Kaisa had shifted on her seat, being conscious of the other boy's gaze on her. But Sirkka had just lifted her eyes towards Lasse and said, 'I'm not sure my boyfriend or Kaisa's fiancé would be very impressed with that.'

Lasse had been silenced, and soon afterwards the pair had left their table and started chatting up two other girls at the back of the restaurant.

'You are terrible! You don't have a boyfriend here do you?' Kaisa had said.

Sirkka had put her hand on Kaisa's. 'For a woman engaged to be married, you can be very naive and inexperienced sometimes. I'm not meeting anyone, and the boys there knew it. I just wanted to let them know we were not worth pursuing, so that they don't waste time on us.'

Kaisa had felt stupid. Of course she knew Sirkka didn't have any friends on the island, but there was a chance she'd met someone before Kaisa arrived.

Sirkka had squeezed Kaisa's hand and said, 'Little sis, don't worry about it. It's good; that's your charm, and that's why every man in this room is making eyes at you right now.'

Kaisa had laughed, 'They're not!' But she'd glanced over to the other side of the restaurant to see if Tom was still there. The bar was empty.

The evening had gone in the same vein as it started at Club Marina; they'd been approached by several groups of men, and when Sirkka had decided she was bored with them, she'd made up an excuse and got the men to go away, or the girls themselves had left the bar. At the late-night disco, Arkipelag, where everyone in the small town of Mariehamn seemed to end their nights out, it'd become more difficult to brush aside approaches. Many of the men were very drunk, and Kaisa had had to slap groping hands. When Sirkka had to threaten an older guy, who could hardly stand up but still thought he could touch Sirkka's knee, with calling one of the bulky security guards who stood outside the disco, the girls decided to call it a night. Kaisa hated the attention she got, but Sirkka just laughed at the stupidity of men.

Now in the taxi, they were both giggling. The darkened landscape was whizzing past them and Kaisa could see occasional glimpses of the sea as the road dipped in and out of the coastline. She loved the dusk in summer; the nights never got properly dark even in Southern Finland, although now, towards the end of July, there was a deepening darkness to the night, which reminded Kaisa of the inevitability of autumn and the long bleak winter ahead.

'Did you see his face, when he saw us?' Sirkka said.

For a moment Kaisa thought she was talking about Tom, and was startled because she hadn't got a chance to tell Sirkka about him. But she realised Sirkka was talking about Lasse, from the Club Marina. The two boys had been in Arkipelag too, and Lasse, the braver of the two, had come over and asked Sirkka where her boyfriend and Kaisa's fiancé were.

'Oh, they had to leave,' Sirkka had said with a straight face, but Kaisa hadn't been able to control a muffled laugh, which Lasse had seen.

'He wasn't pleased you'd lied to him,' Kaisa now said.

'It was for his own good!' Sirkka said.

FOURTEEN

The next day, Kaisa woke up to the sound of birds singing outside the cottage. She opened her eyes and saw it was another beautiful day, without a cloud in the sky. She smiled when she thought she'd have another six mornings to wake up like this, six more lazy days to spend with her mother and sister. She got out of bed and pulled on a pair of jeans and a T-shirt, careful not to wake Sirkka, who was fast asleep on the bed opposite. Barefoot, she tiptoed out of the room and stepped outside when she saw her mother's fair head through the window.

'Good morning, darling.' Pirjo said. She was sitting on a foldable nylon chair on the wooden porch, drinking coffee out of a large white mug. The view of the sea before them was stunning: beyond the band of reeds swaying gently in the breeze, a large sailing boat was slowly making its way out to sea. Kaisa could just make out two shapes on the deck, fiddling with ropes.

Another smaller boat, with a loud motor, was going in the opposite direction. It cut the clear blue surface of the sea in two and created a set of white-topped waves in its wake, the buzzing sound slowly fading into the distance. Beyond the vessels, two islands – one large and wide, one small and tall – broke the perfect line of the horizon.

'Coffee?' her mother asked, and Kaisa nodded. As Pirjo got up and disappeared inside the cottage, Kaisa noticed she had covered the small table with a fresh tablecloth, and set out cups and plates for three. Kaisa smiled and leaned back on the chair. She'd missed her mother.

Pirjo reappeared from the cottage and brought out bread, cheese and ham, and a jug of coffee.

'Here, let me help you,' Kaisa said, as Pirjo struggled with the tray and the door to the cottage.

The two women sat down and silently enjoyed the vista before them while drinking their coffee.

'Not too strong for you?' Pirjo asked.

Kaisa smiled, 'A little, but it's OK. I need it to wake up.'

Pirjo settled her gaze on her daughter and Kaisa saw how beautiful her mother's pale blue eyes were, even without make-up.

'Did you have fun last night?' her mother asked.

'Yes, we did.'

'Meet anyone nice?'

'No, of course not!' Kaisa's words had come out louder than she had intended.

Her mother looked down at her coffee cup, and

Kaisa added, 'Have you forgotten I'm engaged to be married?'

Pirjo lifted her eyes towards her daughter again, 'No ...'

'But what?' Kaisa knew there was a 'but' coming, and anger surged inside her. The offer of a holiday had been a trap after all, to show her what fun it was to be single, to put her in a situation where she might even fall for another man. Was that why Pirjo had decided to stay home last night, to give Sirkka a chance to show Kaisa what she was missing? Kaisa realised that Matti had been right. Not that he'd said it, but she knew he'd thought it. He knew both Sirkka and her mother believed she was too young to be engaged. Kaisa knew they wished she'd see the error of her ways and break it off with Matti. Neither of them had expected the relationship to last the five years it had. Sirkka had gone as far as saying it out loud many times, but so far at least, her mother hadn't expressly told her she should leave Matti. Of course, neither of them understood how well Matti took care of Kaisa. Besides, neither her mother nor Sirkka were in any position to give Kaisa relationship advice. Pirjo had a messy divorce behind her, and Sirkka, well, her sister had had a string of unsuitable boyfriends, and was no expert either. And there was nothing wrong with Matti. On the contrary, he was reliable, well-mannered, from a wealthy family and kind to Kaisa. He was good-looking, in an old-fashioned, Russian way, which was surely romantic?

'I am very happy with Matti,' Kaisa said, emphasising each word.

'Are you? Really?' Pirjo was looking kindly at her daughter, and suddenly Kaisa felt a lump in her throat. Would it be so wrong to admit to her mother that during the past year at Hanken, among people her own age, who seemed to do nothing but go out to parties and flirt with each other in the corridors and the library, she'd begun to wonder if she really was too young to be so tied down. She was the odd one out in Hanken, not only because she was from an ordinary Finnish-speaking family, but also because she was engaged to be married. She remembered telling Tuuli, her new friend, about Matti a few weeks after lectures had started. Tuuli, the tall, confident girl, with a cool, detached manner, had exclaimed in a loud voice, 'What? You got engaged at sixteen!'

Kaisa hadn't seen her react in that way about anything before.

They'd been standing at the bottom of the central staircase in the Hanken main building, and people had turned around to look at Kaisa as if she was a creature from another planet.

Pirjo, now sensing the change in Kaisa's demeanour, leaned over the small table and put her hand on top of Kaisa's, 'There's no shame in changing your mind. You are young, beautiful and talented. You have a great future in front of you with or without Matti.'

Kaisa was fighting tears. 'Yes, I know.'

'And you were too young when the two of you

met. You know it, and Matti, who is so much older than you, should have known it.'

'But, Mum, I can't let him down. I can't go back on my word. And then there's the flat.'

Pirjo took both of Kaisa's hands into hers. 'Darling girl, you have to think about yourself. This is the rest of your life. Don't make the mistake I made, staying with a man you don't love.'

'I do love Matti!' But the words seemed wrong somehow. She felt tears prick her eyes, and wiped them away.

'What's going on here?' Sirkka stood in the doorway, with her hands on her hips, looking from her mother to Kaisa. She was wearing a mustard-coloured, crochet bikini, showing off her bronzed, shapely body.

'We're talking about Matti,' Pirjo said and sighed. 'Coffee?'

'Yes, please.'

Sirkka sat on the steps to the cottage, with her body stretched towards the sun, and her back to Pirjo and Kaisa. Pirjo poured some of the steaming liquid onto a third cup on the table.

'What a view!' Sirkka said, taking the coffee.

When neither Pirjo or Kaisa replied, Sirkka turned around and looked at the two women, 'C'mon, this is a holiday. Let's not talk about men! Especially not Matti!' She grinned at Kaisa and she smiled back at her sister. 'Deal?' Sirkka added.

'Deal,' Kaisa and Pirjo said in unison.

The next day, Sirkka, Kaisa and their mother took the bus into Mariehamn. They needed some provisions and Sirkka said she was bored and needed to get out of the cottage. As they walked along the path up towards the main road, and passed the large house, the farmer waved to them. Bo Gustafsson wore a pair of long shorts and a stripy shirt. He looked tall and lanky, and a little lonely standing outside his house smiling at them. Sirkka nudged their mother, giggling.

'Don't do that; he'll see!' Kaisa's mother said, widening her eyes. She waved elegantly at the man, giving him a quick smile, then turned her head away. Kaisa and Sirkka also lifted their hands in a quick greeting and continued along the path.

'Bo said we should try *Åland's Pannkaka* at Svarta Katten while in town,' their mother said as they stood waiting for the bus by the side of the road.

Both her daughters looked at their mother.

'When did he say that?' Sirkka asked, her eyes wide.

Pirjo smiled smugly, 'Oh, he came around Saturday night while you were out, just to check everything was OK with us and at the cottage.'

Kaisa and Sirkka looked at each other.

'And what happened?' Sirkka said.

'We had a very pleasant chat.'

Their mother wouldn't say a word more about the farmer, or his visit, even though all through the twenty-minute ride into town the girls teased her mercilessly. Their mother seemed to enjoy the teasing, but when they were approaching Mariehamn, Pirjo said, 'That's enough, now girls.'

Sirkka, rolling her eyes, said, 'He's after you, mark my words.'

During the morning the wind had changed direction, and as they walked along the main shopping street, Torggatan, they shivered in their summery clothes. Kaisa had decided on a pair of light cotton pants and a short-sleeved blouse, while her sister was wearing a dress that kept riding up with each gust of wind. Pirjo's white striped dress in a slightly thicker cotton made her look like a local in this seafaring island community. The town was busy with tourists, all equally taken aback by the sudden chill of the wind. All, that is, apart from the sailors who'd stopped over in Mariehamn while touring the archipelago. You could tell these holidaymakers had money; they wore expensive Docker shoes and windbreakers with colourful cotton shorts. The Finns and Swedes who'd come on a day's cruise to drink themselves silly on the tax-free alcohol on the ferries wore flimsy cotton jackets and carried plastic bags advertising the ferry companies they'd used.

Kaisa glanced nervously at the people walking towards them. 'I hope we don't bump into those Finnish boys again,' she said to Sirkka.

'What Finnish boys?' Pirjo asked, her eyes showing her eagerness for gossip about their night out, and getting her own back for the teasing in the bus.

'Oh, just some sailors from Finland who took a liking to Kaisa,' Sirkka said.

'No they didn't!' Kaisa protested, but she couldn't help smiling. 'They were far too young for me,' she added, and immediately regretted her words, in case they thought she was actually looking for someone.

Which she most definitely wasn't.

Neither her mother or Sirkka commented, but she could see they exchanged glances.

Kaisa sighed and seeing a sign for Svarta Katten, the café the farmer had recommended, said, 'There, that's the place,' glad to be able to change the subject.

It was a relief to get out of the northerly breeze, but everyone else had the same idea, because the small café, which was inside an old villa in the centre of town, was packed full of other tourists. They ordered coffee and the recommended delicacy, *Åland's Pannkaka*, a thick oven-baked semolina and egg dessert served with local plum jam, from the self-service counter. Kaisa was carrying the tray of drinks, scanning the second room in the rabbit warren interior, when she saw him.

Tom was leaning back on an old-fashioned sofa. The place was full of ancient, mismatched furniture like some old lady's musty living room. He had one of his arms draped over the back of the seat. His light brown hair was ruffled, as usual, and his blue eyes were looking straight at Kaisa. On his lips was a full smile this time. He was grinning, as if he'd caught Kaisa unawares. Which he had.

Kaisa was rooted to the doorway, but now turned sharply and told her sister, who was behind her holding a tray laden with three plates of the *pannkaka*, 'There's no room.'

Sirkka peered over Kaisa's shoulder and said, 'Yes there is, in the corner, look!' She darted across the room and Kaisa had no choice but to follow. She kept her eyes on the floor, but as she passed his table, Tom leaned across and said, in Swedish, '*Hej, Kaisa!*'

Both Kaisa's mother and Sirkka turned to look at Tom, and now all three women stood in the middle of the busy café staring at the rich boy from Hanken.

Kaisa swallowed hard, and said, '*Hej.*'

She couldn't bring herself to look at the wolfish eyes, and kept her face down.

'What are you doing here?' Tom asked. This was the most he'd said to her in twelve months, since Tuuli and Kaisa had been hit on by the 'rich boys' as they had dubbed the older 'forever students', still in their fourth year at the university. The gang of four boys, who all had wealthy parents, Kaisa supposed, had been studying at Hanken for years. They were known to go out and sleep with as many girls as they could, rather than study. When Tom and his friend Ricky had approached Tuuli and Kaisa during their first weeks at Hanken, both had declined the offer to go out with them. Since then, Kaisa and Tom had been playing a silent game of cat and mouse, each trying to avoid looking at the other, yet always being aware of each other's presence in the student union or library.

Kaisa now lifted her eyes to Tom, but before she could speak her mother came over and took the tray from her. 'Coffee's getting cold,' she said and smiled at Tom.

'Holiday with family,' Kaisa said, gesturing to Sirkka and Pirjo. Her sister and mother, now seated at the corner table, smiled in Tom's direction. Kaisa was grateful there was no sniggering, or whispering.

Tom was sitting on the sofa on his own. There were empty cups of coffee and a plate smeared with jam in front of him.

'Did you enjoy it?' Kaisa said and nodded at the plate, which had obviously contained a piece of *Åland's Pannkaka*.

Tom looked puzzled for a moment and then shook his head, 'No, that's not mine ...'

At that moment, a tall, blond girl came out of a door to the side, which Kaisa suddenly realised was the loo, and smiled confidently at Tom. 'Ready?'

Tom looked from the girl to Kaisa and nodded. He stood up and followed the girl, who had not even acknowledged Kaisa, out of the door. He passed Kaisa so closely she could feel the heat of his body. He stood still for a moment, as if to soak up the sense of their bodies almost touching. He was looking down at Kaisa, reminding her of how tall he was. He gave her his confident smile and said, 'See you.' He glanced at Sirkka and Pirjo who were observing the scene in silence from the corner table, and gave them a nod.

And then he was gone.

FIFTEEN

Helsinki, Summer 1980

Kaisa saw Matti as soon as the double doors out of the arrivals hall at Helsinki airport opened. He was standing erect, with his feet slightly apart, wearing his grey Customs House uniform, a little away from the small crowd of people waiting for their friends or family to emerge from the luggage hall. Kaisa smiled at him, trying to remember that this was her life.

This was Matti, her fiancé, waiting to take her home, whatever her sister and mother had tried to tell her in Åland – she was too young to be engaged, she should enjoy life, she should go after that rich boy Tom. (As if she would, or even could! When she had tried to tell them how bad Tom was, how he slept around and drank and smoked too much, and kept failing his exams, her sister and mother just smiled and said, 'But you could be the one to change him!')

Kaisa knew that they were teasing her, of course, but underlying all those comments was their genuine worry for her. She kept assuring them that she was OK. She loved Matti and was happy to marry him once she'd finished her studies.

All those words and silly discussions with Sirkka and Pirjo in the sauna, or afterwards outside the cottage, while drinking too much wine and watching the sun set into the sea, must be forgotten now. She was a responsible young woman, who would not go back on her word. She had said yes to marriage, and she would hold herself to that.

Smiling, Kaisa walked towards Matti, and into his embrace. When Matti put his full lips on Kaisa's and gave her a long, passionate kiss, she tried to reignite the love she knew she felt for him. But in spite of her best efforts, her thoughts kept going back to a certain wolfish smile.

'Damn that spoiled rich boy, he's not going to ruin me,' Kaisa thought and squeezed Matti closer.

SIXTEEN

'I've missed you,' Matti said, placing his hand on Kaisa's knee. He wanted to ask her about the holiday, about the men she'd met. He glanced sideways at her, while still keeping his eyes on the road. He was a good driver, so he put his hand back onto the wheel and decided to postpone the discussion with his fiancée until they were alone in his room. Kaisa's silence was telling, but Matti tried to keep calm.

'So did you meet many men?' Matti said to the top of Kaisa's head. She was lying in the crook of his arm, almost fully clothed, on his single bed. As soon as they'd got back to his house and had the obligatory coffee and cinnamon buns with his mother, Matti had taken Kaisa's hand and led her upstairs to his room. Brimming over with desire, he'd ripped her knickers off and taken her from behind while she was still wearing her sky-blue dress. It was the dress she'd worn when they got engaged on

Suomenlinna Island, and he'd been glad to see her wearing it when she emerged from the customs hall at Helsinki airport. But then, during the drive, and while they were having coffee, Kaisa had been quieter than usual, saying only a few words about the holiday, and reacting to his mother's questions about her family with monosyllabic replies. Kaisa was usually shy – it was one of the things he loved most about her, but normally, after spending time with her mother and sister, she was animated, almost flamboyant. It was this side of her that Matti didn't like, and the reason he'd tried to discourage contact with Kaisa's mother and sister. This holiday alone with them had been the worst idea, and he'd tried everything in his power to prevent her from going. In the end, Kaisa's assurances that nothing would happen, and the fact that she was paying for the travel herself, had made it impossible for Matti to stop it.

'No, of course I didn't!' Kaisa said, turning her blue eyes on Matti.

'But surely your mother and sister wanted to go out and meet men?' Matti insisted. He knew Kaisa was hiding something, and he was determined to get to the bottom of it.

Kaisa sighed melodramatically, got up, and pulled her knickers back on. Getting a glimpse of her bare, pale buttocks made Matti feel a twinge in his groin. 'Come here,' Matti said and took hold of her arm.

Kaisa let him kiss her mouth, but then wriggled out of his embrace and got up again.

'Look, I'm tired, and I've got to work tomorrow, so can you take me home now?'

Matti replied by putting her hand on his thickening erection, but Kaisa pulled herself away and stood there, looking down at him as if he was the problem. Matti pulled his pants on and picked up the car keys from his desk. 'Yeah, well, I've got some work to do too,' he said, and, looking at Kaisa, added, 'But don't forget your manners; you have to say goodbye to my mother.'

'So what's his name?' Matti asked as soon as they had pulled out of the drive.

Kaisa sighed and turned her face towards Matti. 'Look, there was nobody, I swear!'

Matti said nothing, and didn't even look at her; instead, he put the indicator on and parked the car on the side of the road. He took the keys slowly out of the ignition, and turned to Kaisa, taking hold of her hands. 'I'm not stupid you know. I can tell you've had a good time with your divorced mother and single sister. You are a beautiful girl, and I wouldn't expect anything else. I know men would have been swarming around you like flies, with their tongues hanging out, and you wearing next to nothing.' Here Matti's voice grew hoarse, and his eyes dark. His grip tightened on Kaisa's wrists.

'But I didn't!' Kaisa said. She could feel tears burning behind her eyelids. Matti was hurting her.

Matti was quiet for a moment. Kaisa didn't dare to

look at him; instead, she sat still, not breathing, waiting for him to calm down. Eventually, his grip slackened, and he let go of her. 'You promise?' he said, and lifted Kaisa's chin up with his hand.

Kaisa moved her gaze towards Matti's dark eyes, which looked friendly again, and nodded.

'Good girl,' Matti said and restarted the car.

Kaisa kept herself still all the way to Lauttasaari, trying not to cry. What was wrong with Matti? Why was he so jealous all the time? Had he known how good she'd been, he wouldn't be so suspicious. And why did he have to be so awful about her mother and sister? The snide remarks about them both being single and desperate to meet men, and then the jibe about manners! Kaisa knew full well that Matti's mother thought her family common and a bad influence on her. But she'd thought Matti liked her mother and sister, although Sirkka had always been critical of the seven-year age gap between her and Matti, and often didn't bother to hide her dislike of their engagement. So why was he being awful about them now? She thought back to the nights out in Mariehamn with Sirkka; if she'd only snapped her fingers, she could have had any man there. Well, perhaps not any, not Tom, the rich boy from Hanken, but she certainly could have had her pick at the Arkipelag disco. Matti was right, the men there did have the hots for her. But, because she'd been loyal to Matti, to her fiancé, she hadn't so much as flirted with anyone. Apart from Tom, perhaps. If she was honest with herself, Kaisa knew she'd been disappointed when Tom had left the

Svarta Katten café with the beautiful blonde. What would have happened if he'd been on his own and invited Kaisa out for a drink? Would she have refused? How loyal to Matti would she have been then? Guilt rose up in Kaisa and she looked sideways at Matti, as he finished parking the car outside the block of flats. He leaned over the gearstick to kiss her.

'I'm working nights next week, but I can come over on Saturday.' Matti's eyes were dark, but he didn't look angry anymore, just serious.

Kaisa nodded and thanked him for the ride. She let herself safely inside the building and then watched him drive off through the glass panel in the door. He was a gentleman and always concerned for her safety, Kaisa thought, and smiled. It was barely six o'clock on a Sunday evening in early August, and the Lauttasaari island suburb was deserted, so there was really no need for Matti to be so protective. Still, it was nice of him to be concerned.

However jealous Matti was, it only meant he loved her very, very much.

THE NORDIC HEART BOOKS 1-4

She has her life planned out. He lets the wind guide his sails. As the Cold War heats up, can they keep love alive on either side of the iron curtain?

Finland, 1980. Kaisa has never been a risk taker. After graduation, she plans to marry the dependable older man who helped to pay for her classes and kept a roof over her head. But when she accepts an invitation to a party at the British Embassy, a handsome naval officer makes her want to throw caution to the wind. She surprises herself when they share a passionate kiss under the stars and promise to see each other again. But how could she possibly give up her sure-thing relationship for a man she barely knows?

When Peter Williams pictured his future, he saw a rising in the ranks and an endless trip around the world. Though when he meets the strong-willed Kaisa in Helsinki, his passion for the sea takes a serious turn. Not even the excitement of hunting down Russian submarines can compare to the thrill of his lips on hers. But despite his growing feelings, his commanding officers won't tolerate him pursuing a woman from a Soviet-friendly nation.

Both torn between impossible choices, Kaisa and Peter must search their souls for the right answer. With the Cold War heating up between them, can two star-crossed lovers find their courage or will their relationship sink on the high seas?

The Nordic Heart is a breathtaking contemporary women's fiction series with an undercurrent of romance. If you like vivid historical details, star-crossed chemistry, and complex characters, then you'll love Helena Halme's tale of a Cold War romance.

The Nordic Heart Series

- Prequel The Young Heart
- Book 1 The English Heart
- Book 2 The Faithful Heart
- Book 3 The Good Heart
- Book 4 The True Heart
- Book 5 The Christmas Heart (Out Fall 2018)

Buy *The Nordic Heart Books 1-4* to experience a vibrant tale of courage and love in the face of war today!

Turn over to read the first chapter from *The English Heart*.

THE ENGLISH HEART

CHAPTER ONE

The British Embassy was a grand house on a tree-lined street in the old part of Helsinki. The chandeliers were sparkling, the parquet floors polished, the antique furniture gleaming. The ambassador and his wife, who wore a long velvet skirt and a frilly white blouse, stood in the doorway to the main reception room, officially greeting all guests. When it was Kaisa's turn, she took the invitation, with its ornate gold writing, out of her handbag, but the woman didn't even glance at it. Instead she took Kaisa's hand and smiled briefly, before she did the same to Kaisa's friend Tuuli, and then to the next person in line. Kaisa grabbed the hem of her dress to pull it down a little. When a waiter in a white waistcoat appeared out of nowhere and offered her a glass of sherry from a silver tray, Kaisa nodded to her friend and they settled into a corner of a brightly lit room and sipped the sweet drink.

A few people were scattered around the room, talking English in small groups, but the space seemed too large for all of them. One woman in a cream evening gown glanced briefly towards the Finnish girls and smiled, but most were unconcerned with the two of them standing alone in a corner, staring at their shoes, in a vain attempt not to look out of place.

Kaisa touched the hem of her black-and-white crepe dress once more. She knew it suited her well, but she couldn't help thinking she should have borrowed an evening gown form somewhere.

Kaisa looked at her friend, and wondered if Tuuli was as nervous about the evening as she was. She doubted it; Tuuli was a tall, confident girl. Nothing seemed to faze her.

'You look great,' Tuuli said, as if she'd read Kaisa's mind.

'I keep thinking I should have worn a long dress.' Kaisa said.

Kaisa's friend from university looked down at her own turquoise satin blouse, which fitted tightly around her slim body. She'd tucked the blouse smartly into her navy trousers. On her feet, Tuuli had a pair of light-brown loafers with low heels. Kaisa's courts made her, for once, the same height as Tuuli.

'What did the woman at the bank say, exactly?' Tuuli asked. Kaisa noticed her blue eyes had turned the exact same hue as her blouse. Her friend was very pretty. Students and staff at Hanken, the Swedish language university to which Kaisa had so remarkably gained entry a year ago, thought the two girls were sisters, but Kaisa didn't think she looked anything like Tuuli. As well as being much taller, her friend also had larger breasts, which made men turn and stare.

'Cocktail dresses...' Kaisa replied.

'Well, I don't wear dresses. Ever.' Tuuli had a way of stating her opinion so definitely that it excluded all future conversation on the matter.

'I didn't mean that. You look fantastic. It's just that she was so vague...' Kaisa was thinking back to the conversation she'd had with her boss at the bank where she worked as a summer intern. The woman was married to a Finnish naval officer whose job it was to organise a visit by the British Royal Navy to Helsinki. She had told Kaisa it was a very important occasion as this was the first visit to Finland by the English fleet since the Second World War. 'The Russians come here all the time, so this makes a nice change.' The woman had smiled and continued, 'We need some Finnish girls at the cocktail party to keep the officers company, and I bet you speak good English?'

She was right; languages were easy for Kaisa. She'd lived in Stockholm as a child and spoke Swedish fluently. Kaisa had been studying English since primary school and could understand almost everything in British and American TV series, even without looking at the subtitles. She'd all but forgotten about the conversation when, weeks later, the invitation arrived. Kaisa's heart had skipped a beat. She'd never been inside an embassy, or been invited to a cocktail party. The card with its official English writing seemed

too glamorous to be real. Kaisa now dug out the invite
and showed it to her friend.

*'Her Britannic Majesty's Ambassador and Mrs Farquhar
request the pleasure of the company of Miss Niemi and guest for
Buffet and Dancing on Thursday 2 October 1980 at 8.15 pm.'*

'Whatever, this will be fun,' Tuuli said determinedly
and handed the card back to Kaisa. She took hold of
her arm, 'Relax!'

Kaisa looked around the room and tried to spot
the lady from the bank, but she was nowhere to be
seen. There were a few men whose Finnish naval
uniforms she recognised. They stood by themselves,
laughing and drinking beer.

'Couldn't we have beer?' Tuuli asked.

Kaisa glanced at the women in evening gowns.
None of them were holding anything but sherry.
'Don't think it's very ladylike,' she said.

Tuuli said nothing.

After about an hour, when no one had said a word
to Kaisa or Tuuli, and after they'd had three glasses of
the sickly-tasting sherry, they decided it was time to
leave. 'We don't have to say goodbye to the ambassador and his wife, do we?' Tuuli said. She'd been
talking about going to the university disco.

Kaisa didn't have time to reply. A large group of
men, all wearing Navy uniforms with flashes of gold
braid, burst through the door, laughing and chatting.

They went straight for the makeshift bar at the end of the large room. The space was filled with noise and Kaisa and Tuuli were pushed deeper into their corner.

Suddenly a tall, slim man in a British Navy uniform stood in front of Kaisa. He had the darkest eyes she'd ever seen. He reached out his hand, 'How do you do?'

'Ouch,' Kaisa said and pulled her hand away quickly. He'd given her an electric shock. He smiled and gazed at her.

'Sorry!' he said but kept staring at Kaisa with those eyes. She tried to look down at the floor, or at Tuuli, who seemed unconcerned by this sudden invasion of foreign, uniformed men around them. 'What's your name?'

'Kaisa Niemi.'

He cocked his ear, 'Sorry?' It took the Englishman a long time to learn to pronounce Kaisa's Finnish name. She laughed at his failed attempts to make it sound at all authentic, but he didn't give up.

Eventually, when happy with his pronunciation, he introduced himself to Kaisa and Tuuli, 'Peter Williams.' He then tapped the shoulders of two of his shipmates. One was as tall as him but with fair hair, the other a much shorter, older man. Awkwardly they all shook hands, while the dark Englishman continued to stare at Kaisa. She didn't know what to say or where to put her eyes. She smoothed down her dress, while he took a swig out of a large glass of beer. Suddenly he noticed Kaisa's empty hands, 'May I get you a drink? What will you have?'

'Sherry,' she hated the taste of it, but couldn't think of what else to ask for.

Peter's dark eyes peered at Kaisa intensely. 'Stay here, promise? I'm going to leave this old man in charge of not letting you leave.' The shorter guy gave an embarrassed laugh and the Englishman disappeared into the now crowded room.

'So is it always this cold in Helsinki?' the short man asked. Kaisa explained that in the winter it was worse, there'd be snow soon, but that in summer it was really warm. He nodded, but didn't seem to be listening to her. She tried to get her friend's attention but Tuuli was in the middle of a conversation with the blonde guy.

Kaisa was oddly relieved when Peter returned. He was carrying a tray full of drinks and very nearly spilled them all when someone knocked him from behind. Everyone laughed. Peter's eyes met Kaisa's. 'You're still here!' he said and handed her a drink. It was as if he'd expected her to have escaped. Kaisa looked around the suddenly crowded room. Even if she'd decided to leave, it would have been difficult to fight her way to the door. The throng of people forced Peter to stand close to Kaisa. The rough fabric of his uniform touched her bare arm. He looked at Kaisa. He asked what she did; she told him about her studies at the School of Economics. He said he was a sub-lieutenant on the British ship.

Kaisa found it was easy to talk to this foreign man. Even though her English was at times faltering, they seemed to understand each other straightaway. They laughed at the same jokes. Kaisa wondered if this is what it would be like to have a brother. She had an older sister but had always envied friends with male siblings. It would be nice to have a boy to confide in, someone who knew how other boys thought, what they did or didn't like in a girl. An older brother would be there to protect you, while a younger brother would admire you.

Kaisa looked around what had been a group of them and noticed there was just Peter and her left in the corner of the room. She asked where her friend was. Peter took hold of her arm and pointed, 'Don't worry. I think she's OK.' She saw a group of Finnish naval officers. Tuuli was among them, drinking beer and laughing.

When the music started, Peter asked Kaisa to dance. There were only two other couples on the small parquet floor. One she recognised as the Finnish Foreign Minister and his wife, a famous model, now too old for photo shoots but still envied for her dress sense and beautiful skin. She wore a dark lacy top and a skirt, not an evening gown, Kaisa noticed to her relief. The woman's hair was set up into a complicated do, with a few long black curls framing her face. They bounced gently against her tanned skin as she pushed her head back and laughed at something her minister husband said.

Peter took hold of Kaisa's waist and she felt the heat of his touch through the thin fabric of her dress. She looked into his dark eyes and for a moment they stood motionless in the middle of the dance floor.

Slowly he started to move. Kaisa felt dizzy. The room spun in front of her eyes and she let her body relax in the Englishman's arms.

'You dance beautifully,' he said.

Kaisa smiled, 'So do you.'

He moved his hand lower down Kaisa's back and squeezed her bottom.

'You mustn't,' Kaisa said, not able to contain her laughter. She removed his hand and whispered, 'That's the Foreign Minister and his famous wife. They'll see!'

'Ok,' he nodded and lazily glanced at the other couples on the dance floor.

After a few steps Kaisa again felt his hand drop down towards the right cheek of her backside. She tutted and moved it back up. *He must be very young*, Kaisa thought. When the music stopped, Peter put her hand in the crook of his arm and led her away from the dance floor. He found two plush chairs by a fireplace in a smaller room. It had windows overlooking a groomed garden. As soon as they sat down, a gong rang for food.

'You must be hungry,' Peter said, and not waiting for a reply got up, 'I'll get you a selection.' He made Kaisa promise to stay where she was and disappeared into the queue of people. She felt awkward sitting alone, marking the time until Peter's return. She could feel the eyes of the ladies she'd seen earlier in the evening upon her.

Kaisa smoothed down her dress again and looked at her watch: it was ten past eleven already. She saw

Tuuli in the doorway to the larger room. She was holding hands with a Finnish naval officer, smiling up at him.

Quickly Kaisa walked towards them. 'Are you going? Wait, I'll come with you.' She was relieved that she didn't have to leave alone.

Tuuli looked at the Finnish guy, then at her friend, 'Umm, I'll call you tomorrow?'

Kaisa felt stupid. 'Ah, yes, of course.' She waved her friend goodbye.

Peter reappeared, balancing two glasses of wine and two huge platefuls of food in his hands.

'I didn't know what you liked,' he said, grinning.

He led Kaisa back to the plush chairs. She watched him wolf down cocktail sausages, slices of ham, and potato salad as if he'd never been fed. He emptied his plate and said, 'Aren't you hungry?'

Kaisa shook her head. She wasn't sure if it was the formal surroundings or all the sherry she'd drunk, but she couldn't even think about food. All she could do was sip the wine. She leant back in her chair and Peter sat forward in his. He touched her knee. His touch was like a current running through her body.

'You OK?'

Kaisa felt she could sink into the dark pools of the Englishman's eyes. She shook her head, trying to shed the spell this foreigner had cast over her, 'A bit drunk, I think.'

Peter laughed at that. He put the empty plate away and lit a cigarette. He studied her for a moment. 'You're lovely, do you know that?'

Kaisa blushed.

They sat and talked by the fireplace. The heat of the flames burned the side of Kaisa's arm, but she didn't want to move. While they talked Peter gazed at her intently, as if trying to commit the whole of her being to memory. Kaisa found this both flattering and frightening. She knew she shouldn't be here with this foreign man like this.

Once or twice one of Peter's shipmates came and exchanged a few words with him. There was an Englishwoman he seemed to know very well. He introduced her to Kaisa and laughed at something she said. Then he turned back to Kaisa, and the woman moved away. Kaisa liked the feeling of owning Peter, having all his attention on her. She found she could tell him her life story. He, too, talked about his family in southwest England. He had a brother and a sister, both a lot older than him, 'My birth wasn't exactly planned,' he smiled.

'Neither was mine! My parents made two mistakes, first my sister, then me,' Kaisa said and laughed. Peter looked surprised, as if she'd told him something bad.

'It's OK,' she said.

He took her hands in his and said, 'Can I see you again? After tonight, I mean?'

'Please don't,' she pulled away from his touch.

An older officer, with fair, thinning hair, came into the room and Peter got rapidly onto his feet.

'Good evening,' the man nodded to Kaisa and said something, in a low tone, to Peter.

'Yes, Sir,' Peter replied.

'Who was that?' Kaisa asked.

'Listen, something's happened. I have to go back to the ship.'

Kaisa looked at her watch; it was nearly midnight.

Peter leant closer and held her hands. 'I must see you again.'

'It's not possible.' She lowered her gaze away from the intense glare of his eyes.

'I'm only in Helsinki for another three days,' he insisted.

Kaisa didn't say anything for a while. His hands around hers felt strong and she didn't want to pull away.

'Look, I have to go. Can I at least phone you?'

She hesitated, 'No.'

His eyes widened, 'Why not?'

'It's impossible.' Kaisa didn't know what else to say.

'Why do you say that?' Peter leant closer to her. She could feel his warm breath on her cheek when he whispered into her ear, 'Nothing is impossible.'

People were leaving. Another officer came to tell Peter he had to go. Turning close to Kaisa again he said, 'Please?'

Kaisa heard herself say, 'Do you have a pen?'

Peter tapped his pockets, then scanned the now empty tables. He looked everywhere, asked a waiter carrying a tray full of glasses, but no one had a pen. Kaisa dug in her handbag and found a pink lipstick. 'You can use this, I guess.'

Peter took a paper napkin from a table and she scrawled her number on it. Then, with the final bits of lipstick, he wrote his name and his address on HMS *Newcastle* on the back of Kaisa's invitation to the party.

Outside, on the steps of the embassy, all the officers from Peter's ship were gathered, waiting for something. The blonde guy Kaisa and Tuuli had met earlier in the evening nodded to her and, touching his cap, smiled knowingly. She wondered if he thought she and Peter were now an item. She could see many of the other officers give her sly glances. It was as if outside, on the steps of the embassy, she'd entered another world – the domain of their ship. As the only woman among all the men, she felt shy and stood closer to Peter. He took this to be a sign, and before she could stop him, he'd taken off his cap and bent down to kiss her lips. He tasted of mint and cigarettes. For a moment Kaisa kissed him back; she didn't want to pull away.

When finally Peter let go, everybody on the steps cheered. Kaisa was embarrassed and breathless.

'You shouldn't have done that,' she whispered.

Peter looked at her and smiled, 'Don't worry, they're just jealous.' He led her through the throng of people and down the steps towards a waiting taxi.

'I'll call you tomorrow,' he whispered and opened the car door.

When the taxi moved away, Kaisa saw Peter wave his cap. She told the driver her address and leant back in the seat. She touched her lips.

ALSO BY HELENA HALME

THE CHRISTMAS HEART

Tall, dark and handsome, Tom is out to have some fun. With his beloved mother passed, he's forced to leave his two teenage sons in Milan with his ex, their Italian mother, and is looking forward to an uncomplicated Christmas skiing in the Swedish Alps.

With her daughter Rosa away pack-packing in the Far East, Kaisa decides to take a rare winter break over the holidays with her best friend Tuuli. Now in her late fifties, Kaisa doesn't think she'll ever fall in love again. But when she sees Tom after some thirty years, her heart begins to beat a little faster. Kaisa knows, however, an affair with Tom will go nowhere. Years ago, they had a disastrous date, which neither of them wish to revisit.

Yet, on the slopes and in the apres-ski bars Tom

showers Kaisa with his attentions and she finds she cannot resist his intense eyes and passionate kisses.

Can Kaisa trust this European Casanova, and her own sudden infatuation?

The Christmas Heart is a seasonal story of grown-up love set in the beautiful snow-capped Swedish Alps. It's the final book in the acclaimed *Nordic Heart* romance series, but can also be read as a stand-alone story.

This Nordic Christmas book of second chance love and romance will be out late autumn 2018.

COFFEE AND VODKA

Eeva doesn't want to remember. But now she's forced to return to Finland and confront her past.

'In Stockholm everything is bigger and better.'

When Pappa announces the family is to leave Finland for a new life in Sweden, 11-year-old Eeva is elated. But in Stockholm Mamma finds feminism, Eeva's sister, Anja, pretends to be Swedish and Pappa struggles to adapt.

And one night, Eeva's world falls apart.

Fast forward 30 years. Now teaching Swedish to foreigners, Eeva travels back to Finland when her beloved grandmother becomes ill. On the overnight ferry, a chance meeting with her married ex-lover, Yri, prompts family secrets to unravel and buried memories to come flooding back.

It's time for Eeva to find out what really happened all those years ago ...

Coffee and Vodka has it all: family drama, mystery, romance and sisterly love.

Pick up *Coffee and Vodka* to discover this brilliant, heartwarming Nordic family drama today!

THE RED KING OF HELSINKI

He's a rookie spy chasing a violent Russian KGB man. She's a young student looking for a friend who has mysteriously disappeared. Can he save her?

It's the height of the Cold War and Finland is the playground of the Russian KGB.

A former Royal Navy officer Iain is asked to work undercover. He's to investigate Vladislav Kovtun, a violent KGB spy, dubbed The Red King of Helsinki by the Finnish secret service. This is Iain's first assignment, and when he discovers the bodies left in Kovtun's wake, he quickly gets embroiled in danger.

Young student Pia has two goals in life: she dreams of a career in gymnastics and she wants Heikki, a boy in her class with the dreamiest blue eyes, to notice her.

But when her best friend, Anni, the daughter of an eminent Finnish Diplomat, goes missing, Pia begins to investigate the mystery behind her disappearance.

Unbeknown to Pia, Kovtun, The Red King of Helsinki, is watching her every move, as is the British spy, Iain. Will Iain be able to save Pia before it's too late?

If you like Nordic Noir, you will love this fast moving Nordic spy story by the Finnish author Helena Halme.

DID YOU ENJOY THE YOUNG HEART?

If you enjoyed *The Young Heart*, please leave a review! Reviews are very important to other readers, but they are also vital in making a book visible online, and a huge bonus to the author's writing career.

Go to Amazon or Goodreads to write a review now.

Thank you!

ABOUT THE AUTHOR

Helena Halme grew up in Tampere, central Finland, and moved to the UK via Stockholm and Helsinki at the age of 22. She is a former BBC journalist and has also worked as a magazine editor, a bookseller and, until recently, ran a Finnish/British cultural association in London.

Since gaining an MA in Creative Writing at Bath Spa University, Helena has published seven fiction titles, including five in *The Nordic Heart* Romance Series.

Helena lives in North London with her ex-Navy husband and an old stubborn terrier, called Jerry. She loves Nordic Noir and sings along to Abba songs when no one is around.

You can read Helena's blog at www.helenahalme.com, where you can also sign up for her *Readers' Group*.